THE LUCKY BODY

by

KYLE COMA-THOMPSON

DOCK STREET PRESS

SEATTLE

Spring in Zurveyta first appeared in Bat City Review

www.dockstreetpress.com

ISBN: 978-0-9910657-0-7

Printed in the U.S.A.

For Ahab Cloud, Hamza de Sade, & Mia

CONTENTS

THE LUCKY BODY

PART 1

THE LUCKY BODY

After they shot the body several times, they cut its throat with a scaling knife; after that, they pinched its nostrils and funneled sulfuric acid into its mouth; while some set to yanking the body's toenails out with a set of pliers, others fashioned a noose from a utility cord they had found in the trunk of their car. After murdering it beyond all recognition, they hanged it.

Before the bullets had their say, and the knife, the body had been a handsome brown-haired white adult male of lean build, standing at a height of 6'1". From the way it was dressed they could tell it had elegant manners. It might have attended one of the better boarding schools in the upper Northeast, but since then had gained a measure of worldliness, having sprinted through college and burst through the paper target of its diploma into the wilder terrain of the status-mongering world. A series of women had loved the body for its many perfections, but also for the gentleness with which it was inhabited: the warmth coming off its naked length, nights they lay beside it was a true warmth. Never mind the trickle of some dislodged indiscretion or disagreement had gained in size and force as it plowed down from the heights of their romance to bury them—the avalanche was worth the trouble. The body was kind to them. It had treated them as if they were an extension of itself, and from the openness and understanding with which it explained its feelings they learned just how different men's bodies were from their own; how, though less complex in many ways, with their ridiculous genitals and frank hairiness, were harder to grasp for the very fact of their exclusivity and foreignness.

But this body had not made them feel any lonelier for not understanding, and this made all the difference.

Now the body was bleeding. Though its heart had stopped hours ago, blood still sprang from its flesh as they hammered a nail into its cheek or drew a razor blade across its nipple. After all the abuse they had invested in it, it was still there—as intact as it was the day it had been born. One of them stood over the rest as they worked and voiced his admiration: here's someone who truly wanted to live; just look at how well he holds together.

At this rate they would have to pry him apart cell by cell with tweezers, under a microscope. It had taken thirty seconds to apply mortal damage to the body, surprising it on its way to work, catching a plastic grocery bag over its head and holding it there as the others pounded the contents with a length of pipe, a tire iron, and a crowbar. Nearly half the objects in a domestic setting could be used to achieve a fatal blow, so, as if determined to exhaust their options, they grabbed anything they could put their hands on—any belongings a lesser criminal would simply steal—and these, they threw at him. It was as if they were testing the reality of the objects by throwing them. The bruises and cuts left by their impact were evidence of the ongoing reliability of the physical world. The body lay there as a witness. As proof, it didn't move.

Soon they were exhausted from the effort involved, in the task of killing and rekilling the body. Some had to take a seat while the others kept stabbing and kicking and slashing at it. Soon they agreed to work in shifts. While some slept, others would pick up where they'd left off and continue to inflict damage. The body, being dead, didn't need to sleep or eat, and in that outstripped their stamina. It had nothing living to keep appeased or alive. Unlike them, who had to break from the act to eat a sandwich or massage the soreness in their arms and lower backs and wrists. Killing was difficult work to extend beyond the normal hours of a workday, but the body, it was still there—they had long ago resolved to remove it from the company of the living. So what could they do but keep to their task despite the irreparable wear and tear it was demanding?

Here was a body unlike the others. They had never beaten one quite like it. Its durability, its unassuming congeniality and composure… it lie there without any sign of struggle, more forgiving of its fate and worsening condition than any of them would have been. Surely there must have been parents somewhere far in the depths of its brain matter who had once loved it, raised it with sureness and generosity, without friction of any inner conflict; who had borne it out of their own bodies and fed and clothed it as their own; and borne it brothers and sisters for whom it felt a sense of protectiveness and responsibility; and when it came time to be a grown body, alone in meeting the steep challenges of an adult working life, they sent money when he needed it and always words of encouragement. The body had walked this earth as one of the lucky, and because of that an ineffable glow radiated from every part of it, and it was this they spotted one day and followed for three blocks and admiring it made plans to eventually snatch it off the streets and mine it for what they imagined was its hidden gold.

But opening its guts with a pair of scissors they had found only a mass of bloody brownish entrails. The same grimy mess they would find in any of them. Maybe this was a trick, they thought, maybe the gold wasn't hidden in the body's belly but through a series of internalized deflections had only appeared to glow from beneath its navel. They set about smashing the body's skull open with a hammer. Brains spilled open between their knees like co-agulated oatmeal. Tearing it with their fingers they found nothing. In a rage they stamped on the body's sternum until it cracked, then, with bare hands, yanked both halves of the ribcage open. It was the same as with the head and belly, nothing. Handfuls of viscera, heart and lungs, spleen, kidneys, liver, intestines upper and lower flew over their shoulders, but after all that frantic effort they were still left with what they'd begun with—a man, maybe age thirty-five, of average weight and height in the shape of a body.

What else was left? Where else could they search? As before, the body lay at their feet. Barely recognizable, but to whom? To them? Because they could still remember how fresh and frank it was in its youth, days ago, weeks ago, years ago, when they had first accosted it on the street, dragged it behind a dumpster and beaten it into a condition of meekness and carried it from the alley to their car. Was this the body they had first noticed long ago on that bright spring day when they were walking along, looking for something to destroy and had seen him, this man, this person, this body, re-laxed, calm and boyish, stand from the bench where he'd been sit-ting, to wave at someone they didn't turn around to see coming? Maybe, maybe not. It seemed so long ago now, they could hardly be held accountable if they couldn't remember.

VESNA

Years later he'll wish he'd taken a photograph of them with his camera phone, lying in bed, sheets bundled to their necks to stay warm. It'd been the one night they'd slept together, something neither of them seemed to regret, but the fact that they never did again made him think it might not have happened: that they hadn't been drunk and bored and in one another's company at a bar he can't remember the name of now, their friends all pairing off back into the couples they were, leaving them with the younger crowd who drank and laughed louder. They were both older than any of them by ten years. Not something they joked about but something they noticed, like the surprising outcome of some long, tedious experiment. It felt good, slightly noble to be older. Neither of them felt particularly desperate or lonely; if anything they sat there like serene hallucinations of their daytime habits: working, caring for parents, balancing their meager budgets. They were out of play—no eyes looking. No promise of adventure here. It came as a relief to Vesna, a beautiful woman by nature if not by choice. It took so much less an effort to heighten her best qualities before she left the house for an evening—a little mascara, that's it. Usually jeans and a nice top were enough to draw eyes like flies around her. Part of her charm was how she'd brush them away as if they were hardly worth noticing. Fynn was a different case entirely. Just a quick glance his way and you could see his neuroses coursing through him. Legs stiffly crossed, heel to knee, knees jutting at right angles—one sight of him and you felt uncomfortable. The ways in which he noticed himself caused you to do the same, and the whole lopsided cycle of thinking, judging, looking left you exhausted and overjoyed to just look away, sip your drink mindlessly. That night, though, he'd found that rare pocket of ease which sometimes appeared after the third drink, and suddenly his obvious faults lifted: Vesna looked at him and said, why not, he actually seems kind of cute now, and kissed him.

They were standing outside to the left of the awning. Only when a thin stream of water drizzled on the back of his neck did he realize, oh, it's raining. Vesna lived four blocks from the bar and for her this was a first, to ask someone to walk her home. Appeal to a guy's chivalry, if he has any, then very coyly ask him up to your apartment—knowing how dense Fynn was, she smiled all the way. He couldn't help but see half an hour into the future, both of them making a miniature storm in her bed. Which is what happened. They lost their equilibrium while undressing each other and dropped jack-kneed to the mattress. Kiss kiss kiss. Sex sex sex. Then the two of them lying face up blank as the ceiling and happy. No shame in calling it that: any person over thirty-five in a state of satiation, no matter how brief, is happy.

Then, after she brought waters back for them, from the kitchen, they began talking. Fynn described Bangladesh, where he spent his childhood. Vesna talked about the mindlessness of computer programming. They laughed over the foibles of their friends. They spoke about the weirder things they'd seen, which by the time they'd reached each other in bed had been polished over and over and had accomplished the archetypal gleam of seasoned stories. Fynn told her the story of the house he saw every morning from the Blue Line, in Chicago. For some reason, all year round, every pigeon in the neighborhood seemed drawn to it, so its shingles and gutters were stacked with scat, its aluminum siding white with streaks. Hundreds of them roosted on the roof and he always wondered why. Until one day an old woman sitting next to him caught him watching and told him. "Pigeon Man lives there. Tosses feed up there for them every morning." Vesna chuckled in her water, then handed him the glass.

"That reminds me of something when I was younger," she said, "When my sister and I lived in Croatia." Then she told him about the man who had made her so sad she avoided being touched for a year. "That summer Sasha and I went to Dalmatia, to swim and lay on the beach, we got jobs at a fruit stand and on our off hours biked around town and smoked pot and played volleyball with our friends. There were dozens of beaches near town, and by the middle of summer we'd ridden our bikes down to each, except one, a nude beach, it took us a while to visit that one because our friend Lina was always saying no, she didn't want to go there, too many old men ogling her. But one day Lina was working so Sasha and I said, why not, and went there. It was a nice day, and the beach, it was nice, not too many people there. We laid out our blankets early and watched the boats off the coast. The sand was soft, I mean, it was actually sand, not pebbles like you'd find on most of the beaches. Neither of us had any problem stripping down, but by mid-afternoon there were dozens of people around, the parking lot was full, and there were still more coming on their bikes, actually pedaling into the parking lot naked. Sasha and I were covering our mouths the whole day, laughing. Most of the people there were tourists, Germans and Russians. And not many were old either! Young couples—strong blonde types, the women with enormous serious-looking breasts. But we're Europeans, you know, we're not bothered by that kind of thing. Naked is naked. We spent maybe another hour sipping water flipping through magazines. Sasha walked into the ocean and threw a ball with a few other people. It didn't take long for you to forget you didn't have any clothes on. In fact, it was funny to look through the magazine and see so many people *not* naked!

"I remember I was reading an article about a movie star who had suffered a breakdown at Cannes earlier that summer, had crushed a bunch of tranquilizers and mixed them with gobs of shaving cream and then rubbed the whole mess in his hair. Something about it melting in the sun and streaking down his face in this horrific way—the photos showed him bent over his beer at a sidewalk café, the stuff covering his face like melted wax. He looked like a thousand year old man with a face made of pudding. Sasha had stood up to rub more lotion on her legs. As I held the magazine up to show her the photo I was confused at how scared she looked, though she wasn't looking at the photo but over it, over my shoulder, at something from the parking lot. It was then I turned around and saw him: the man with burns all over his body. He was naked, carrying his trunks and a bottle of water, and his skin shined either because it had healed that way, taut, hairless enough it could reflect sunlight, or because he had rubbed some kind of ointment on it. I had met a man once, a friend of our father's, whose arm had been badly burned during the war, and it had that same kind of shine to it. Since the pores had been fused, he told us, he couldn't sweat, so he was forever having to rub a moisturizing ointment on it. It cooled him off and kept the skin from drying and cracking. But this man, he had burns all over him, head to foot. He wore nothing but sunglasses, the reflector types, aviator glasses, and I couldn't breathe for a full minute after I turned my head away and he walked past us.

"He didn't have a towel, he didn't set up on the beach but just stood there, a few feet from the water, and it was horrible for everyone, I imagine, especially for the ones who were out in the water because he just stood there staring out over it. People began to leave, gradually. The ones who left early left quickest, but the others like us couldn't be so obvious. The fewer people, the clearer the reason why they were picking up and leaving. Sasha and I sat there waiting for the other to get up. But neither of us wanted to be the first to let him know he was disturbing us, even if he was just standing there, his back to us.

"After an hour we put our swimsuits back on, but slowly. He didn't look around, I remember that much, maybe he was shy or ashamed, but when Sasha and I finally stood and gathered up our blankets, a Russian couple came out of the ocean and nodded at him. They'd been swimming back and forth along the water for a while, waiting to see if the man would leave, and when it was clear he wouldn't they walked over to where their clothes were, next to where the man was standing. They spoke briefly, the woman barely looking at him. Her boyfriend or husband, though, stood between them tensely, smiling and talking. It was clear he was forcing himself to look at him. The burned man also smiled but then I realized, no, he had no upper lip, his teeth were just exposed like that, and it was the kind of realization you actually feel run right through your body. When the Russian couple came off the beach we followed them. When Sasha and I stood up our bikes and pedaled out of the parking lot, he was still standing there, no one else on the beach, the water rippling towards him.

"It bothers me now to even think about him. To have skin like that, like chewed bubblegum—who would love you, much less get up the nerve to touch you?" Vesna rubbed her face with both hands then dropped her arms beside her. The sheets were warm and they touched all down the length of their sides: her right, his left. They waited the appropriate time before changing the subject. It was during that time he had his thought: if only I had my phone nearby I'd hold it over us, take a photo. Send it to her next time she feels like crying. But no, it was in his pants pocket, on the floor. The room was too cold for that, it'd be too much trouble to dig for it.

pG

It was not that it was merely bad, this much lauded, frequently name-checked painting, but that it was a travesty, a massive lie, a smear against the very events it would supposedly honor as its subject matter, this famous work of the middle period of (according to Cabernet-sippers and sharp-nosed critics both) the past century's Most Important Painter, polymathic in his ambitions if not always in his abilities, a genius of cartoonish manipulation of organic form, born in Spain but long settled in France, wealthy, unassailable in authority, raised high on a pedestal of envy, a dildo applied by lesser talents when they cannot summon the requisite hardness or girth or length to penetrate a blank canvas, no, their canvases, the canvases of lesser talents shall remain blank forever, while his shall live on and grow like spectacular mold to one day infest the whole House of Art, even in its late convalescence, even as a minor American imitator of several of his fourth generation imitators sits up at night, one particular night in the early years, at the poorly lit depths of a new millennium, sipping a tumbler of bourbon, the whole

room lit by the light of successive bourbons, an American artist, as
he would call himself, or had been in the habit of calling himself,
not without a heavy thumb of irony pressed down upon his
wounded vanity, a very, *very* minor artist, so minor he never actually got around to beginning, who somehow in the messy effort to
make a living had forgotten that one also had to apply that living to
some kind of higher vocation, that is, applying brushes dipped in
paint upon freshly stretched or unstretched canvas, so that one day
he was suddenly beyond the age when anyone could still call him
an apprentice, though he was certainly not a master of anything,
not even of what filled most of his days, that is, attending the needs
and concerns of seventy-four tenants, being a superintendent of a
medium sized building in Manhattan, more busy than he had ever
thought he would be, when he saw the ad, he didn't call the number, he walked over in his only jacket and tie and introduced
himself, passed the three required interviews in quick succession
and found himself thoroughly employed and earning the first
respectable wage of his life, hard to walk away from, even when the
ideas that never came with much frequency stopped coming, so in
that way one year passed comfortably into another, until it was four
years, four exhausting, somewhat happy but in retrospect empty
years, and one day he's walking back from the corner mart when
what should he come across but a sidewalk display, a swivel rack of
postcards, each bearing a reproduction of some masterpiece from
the past five centuries, *five centuries*, it made him almost gasp, *was
modern art so young*, and just as he was marveling at that, applying
just the right amount of unconscious pressure to push down the
dull swell of bad feelings that welled up in him at such moments,

he came across a small reproduction of that famous painting, in color, though that certainly must have been an ironic touch on the part of the publisher, since the painting itself was not only huge but composed of a neutral palate of blacks and grays and whites, in this case the most dramatic possible choice of colors, considering the subject matter, the destruction by the Nazi Luftwaffe of a small village in northern Basque country, the whole village in flames and in full view of the Bay of Biscay, and who knows what it had been like to be there, to smell the burning flesh and embers and hear the shrieks and incomprehensible wailings, doubly incomprehensible since he doesn't know Spanish, and even if he did, how changed even that tongue would be in the dialect of northern Basques, but as he sat studying the painting in its diminished form, small enough to fit into a hand and so be held up to a desk lamp light for inspection, between sips of bourbon, no, this wasn't a war at all, as it was intended to be, or so he assumed, but a painting, and as evidence for that failure one only had to notice the random hash of personal archetypes the painter had thrown together in such a large space, a 7X11 rectangle meant to contain, in frozen record, the totality of a day's suffering, long smoothed over by the consolations of time and civil landscaping, for hadn't he seen these figures before, the bull, the horse, the men and women, some vaguely nude but all contorted, as if ground through the machinations of an idiosyncratic but highly self-conscious aesthetic, their mangled and angular structures more whimsical reflections on his own original view of nature, perhaps even assertions of his power over it, and hence, how could it be otherwise, over them, he felt giddy with disgust, a commanding, irreproachable revulsion at the failure of a great man's self-serving effort, to aggrandize himself at the expense of his countrymen, who, let's be honest, were no more his countrymen than the collectors who bought his art and so ensured his relative comfort during the war years, how much of an insult it was to actual suffering, a doodle on the face of history, minor non-artist that he was, he felt, for the first time in his life, a strong compulsion to right an incorrect reality, a drive to create was at last commanding him, its dictates, though obscure, were undeniable, he would learn with more concentration and determination that he'd ever applied to anything, to become someone open to mysterious discipline, to save money, to skip meals, take a second job, then, once enough has been earned to cover the most basic costs, to purchase a ticket to Barcelona, and from there rent a car, to drive to northeastern Spain, to that place, that very village, now a moderately-sized town, perfectly respectable, and except for a few commemorative plaques and statues, innocent of past horrors, and once there, he would rent a house, one with a large studio-sized garage, and once settled would sit, sit for hours, days, allow the energy amassed by inactivity to concentrate and harden until his whole body took on a secret, lucid glow visible only to him and the depths of certain mirrors, and then would come the time, to go out, out into the town once a village, out into the subject of a great man's failed painting, to select his own materials, though what would those be, he would have to see, he would have to go with total faith in the possibilities of what that instinct would bring back, and that evening, after ten hours trolling the alleyways, he found out, several dozen stray dogs, he was surprised to find them all, and just as he was about to ask what it is he should do with them, the instinct, lucid, cold, told him, kill them, and so he did, the voice returned, hard and clear, dismember them, which he did, and erected onto a large wire mesh frame cut to the exact dimensions of the Great Painting itself, a bloody mess of tooth and fur, affixed to the frame with razor wire, and once finished he stood for some time before a mirror at his bloody self and knew tomorrow he would rise early and do the same, it was what art required of him, so he did, but the next evening it was vagrants, and the evening after, tourists, and after that, policemen, cab drivers, old women he found wandering away from the open air market, each arriving in their own time and incorporated into his painting, if you call it that, perhaps better termed a mixed-media installation, anyone he came across he snared and brought back to his studio, to kill, dismember and affix in gory collage to the frame, which by this time had become cluttered, weighed down in parts, not entirely balanced where it stood, on rollers, so that by the time of its completion it could be seen wobbling slightly, emitting an horrible stink, so many of its materials already rotting, others still bleeding, the whole composition so cluttered it was difficult to take in at one glance, in such a confined space, so according to the dictates of instinct, he opened the garage, rolled the work out into open air, for the first time on public display, with the title written on a small tag tied to the top of the frame, hanging from a length of string so if a breeze were to come by it would flutter, while the rest attracted the attention of various carrion birds and flies, the whole neighborhood in that town of sixteen thousand empty, and that emptiness lacking a specific human noise, which one could also attribute to the artwork, that it could be the cause of the very quiet it contains, calmly bearing the products of inspiration to the only public it would ever need, the title, of course, *Picasso (by Guernica).*

A WILD ONE

"There wasn't just one girl there, there were two," Claude told us. "That'd been my problem, I'd been thinking there was only one. She introduced herself as one person then later turned into another." He was telling us the story of his drive back to a woman's place the previous weekend. He'd been drinking at the Buckle after work on Friday and began sharing beers with her. A tall, thick-legged blonde. She was plain and direct: not a speck of mystique on her.

"She told me her ride had left while we were talking so I said, sure, I could give her a ride home. Really I'd been hoping for that anyway. I'm not young, these kinds of invitations don't come my way often as they used to. And even then!" We chuckled. Right before our eyes began to roll, he saved us the trouble and mocked his own prowess. "She'd been sitting pretty close so I thought, maybe that's an indicator. Walking to my car we kept bumping into each other and she leaned on the car while I dug for my keys. I was having trouble so she leaned in, reached into my jean pocket, right here" (pointing to his right front pocket) "and squirreled around there a bit before wriggling them out. That was it. I was sold. I was on the program. She dangled them before me like they were something really delicious and I let them hang there for a bit catching light off the streetlights before I opened my hand and let her lower them right there on my palm" (his one hand wide open, the fingers of the other making like keys and lowering softly into it). "After that I didn't need any more assurances. I was good to go.

"She said she lived on the West End past Winchester Road. It was about two in the morning. The streets were wet so I guess it must have rained a little while we were at the Buckle. She asked if I like the radio and then turned it on even before I could answer—and the answer would have been, I'd like it just fine, if you're listening to it. She finds a rock station and turns it way up and rolls down her window and tells me to roll down mine and then tells me to sing along with her. One of the songs sounded like the Rolling Stones, but I didn't know it, so I did my best Jagger imitation anyway. After about two songs I look over and, I swear to you now, she was in the middle of taking off her bra. Underneath her shirt. Leaned forward, unhooked it around her back then drew her arms up her sleeves and started wriggling them off her shoulders. One of the arms pulled out of the sleeve holding it by the end—a bright pink one, with shiny, solid-looking cups. She wagged it in my face then threw it in the glove compartment and closed it. I don't have to tell you I was hard as a bullet by then. But that didn't compare with what she did next.

"When we reached the Mission Bridge off Water Street, she told me to hang a right. There's a skinny little street off to the right where the bridge cuts over the tobacco warehouse, Southwest

Tobacco, the one your brother works at, Mike" (nods at Mike, Mike mumbles 'sure'). "I pull off there then slow down because it drops off on a pretty steep short hill and before I can get to the bottom I see movement out the corner of my eye and sure enough, this one, she's wriggled out of her jeans and is working her shirt over her head. It's warm out, but with the windows down it's chilly enough and I'm laughing because I sure couldn't have predicted this. When we hit the street at the bottom, she says, 'right, honey,' and before I'm even off that way she's working the socks off her feet. Those go in the glove compartment, mind you, not like the shirt or jeans, because she throws those out the window! I hit the brakes but she yells with a big smile and tells me to keep going, so you can bet at this point I am sure as hell going to keep going. She's in nothing but her drawers by then and I see her working to get a little silver necklace from around her neck, then she puts that in her throwing hand along with the bracelets around her wrists and chucks those too. One pings a Yield sign while we pass it and I'm laughing and asking 'what the hell?' but she's still just singing along to the music in this goofy voice I suppose is supposed to sound like whoever's singing and then she starts singing, 'Next left, take it…next left, take it', pointing with pointer fingers that way, so off I go that way into a place I'd heard about before, Fruitland Parks, that trailer park where one of those Mexican guys who worked with us a few years ago lived. The streets all named for different fruits, and this one, the one she has me going down is Crabapple, and she's rubbing her hands and feet together, a bit cold by then and sings me another right and two more short lefts, until we find ourselves at the end of a street, lights out on all the porches around us. I'm glad to get the car stopped, but before I can turn to get hold of her she's already pulled herself out the open window, barefoot and running to a chain link fence at the end of the street. She takes that fence like an Olympic hurdler and just lifts herself over in one quick pull and leap. I stand there in front of my car for a minute but jump the fence too and jog down the grass hill there to the edge of what looks like a short cliff, man-made, probably an old rock quarry. And when I finally get there, at the edge where she's standing buck naked, panties tossed, she turns to me like a policeman with her hand out and stops me just short of her and yells, 'Strip!'

"Any of you ever stripped?" (no one nods yes, but no one nods no either) "Well let me tell you, it's not easy to do alone, not to mention while drunk, and even harder in the company of a woman who's already looking really good and naked and is clearly just flat out laughing at you. There's nothing of grace about it. I guess I was going too slowly or was fumbling too much because halfway through she begins reaching out and tugging the clothes right off me. My jeans are at my ankles and I guess that was all she could stand because she pushed me hard right on my ass and went to town on them, yanked them off quick, taking the socks with them. Then she stooped down, gathered all my clothes together and—threw them over the edge! Right off the dark edge of that damn quarry. And I didn't hear the sound of anything striking bottom either! I'm telling you, it's not easy getting angry when you're standing there in the cold with a hard-on! She just laughed at me and tried to grab at me and give me a tug and I covered myself and backed off. When I sidestepped her to look over the edge and see if I could spot anything down there, I guess I could hear her footsteps because she had already taken off, running bare-assed and laughing up the hill. I wasn't thinking any of this was funny anymore but I have to say, for some reason I wasn't really angry either. If there was a warm bed at the end this, what's the complaint?

"So I took off after her. By the time I was at the fence I could see what she was after, she was leaning in the driver's window to fish out the car keys and then she reared up and gave me this look, like she was holding ten grand in cash between her knees, waved real drunk-like and took off to the nearest trailer, padded up the stairs, opened the door and bam, shut it. I was pissed now. I went and knocked on the door and on flipped the floodlight. I knocked softer but of course, I knew by then, no one was going to answer. I tried talking through the door, tried looking in the nearest window, but a porch light across the way came on and I saw someone pull back the curtains and toss them closed again. That's right, up a creek, just like the rest of the shit!" (everyone is laughing by now, at him, with him) "So what do I do?

"I run over holding my wiener and fish that bra and socks from the glove compartment and run back and knock on the window and wave them up there right where she can see them, if she's looking. I even ball one of those socks up and give it a good hard chuck against the window, but nothing. When I come back cursing, with the one sock and bra, the one I tossed lost down in the crack between the porch and trailer, there are two people standing out on their porches, hesitant and pissed-looking, and a third person stepping off his porch toward me. It's a big guy with a mustache and he's telling me his wife is dialing the cops and I'd better get my pervert ass out of their cul-de-sac, and I'm saying that lady who lives over there in that trailer took my car keys and chucked my clothes, but they're yelling too loud at me to hear me. I tell him, 'Give me some clothes and I'll get out of here, I swear' but he says 'I ain't giving you my clothes', and I remember that Southwestern blanket tucked over the leather of the backseat, so I reach over and grab that and wrap myself up and step out of the car because now there's about a half dozen guys telling me to. And what do they do? They walk me down to the end of their street then down the other, all the way back to that road we'd first turned off of. And they stand there shoulder to shoulder and tell me they'd be happy to wait until the cops get here, or I can just get, and when I begin to pad off, they yell at me to run. So I run. No fooling" (everyone is laughing now, not with him, at him). "I ran naked in a blanket like a pig in a blanket, until I reached the top of that hill, and when I reached Water Street I thought, 'Why stop' and so kept going. I tried to hitch a ride, but who'd stop for a guy wrapped in a blanket? I ran until I was about frozen solid but also sweating, and I was shrunken to about the size of a thumbnail. After a few miles, I slowed it down a bit, and just when I was about to get back into town, down by the Ajax Building, what do you think I saw, what do you think I saw coming? That girl and two or three others, in a car, my car, waving their bras forty miles an hour out the window, shouting along to some stupid song I probably didn't know the words to anyway."

SPRING IN ZURVEYTA

Mr. Cherkeso had agreed: he would sit for the interview. It would be conducted at his compound in Zurveyta at exactly 3:45 in the afternoon. The journalist, Ms. Petrovich, would submit a list of questions. From this list ten questions would be selected and his representatives would submit a copy of his answers one hour before the interview. She would be allowed to formulate supplementary questions to his answers during this time. Arrival time would be at noon, granting a thorough search of her car and body; after the interview, they would have dinner with the Minister of the Interior and his wife.

Anna Petrovich, Anna P. as her friends called her (her editor at *Novaya Gazeta*, Mischa Hosculman, called her Petrovich—the negation of familiarity belying his affection for her) had reported on the wars in Khruekistan and predicted the consolidation of power by Akhmed Cherkeso's son after his assassination two years ago. His son had been the head of security forces. He wasn't yet thirty years old when his father had died. This is how it had happened: at a public Independence Day rally at Iznek Stadium, he'd sat in the twenty-fifth row of the concrete bleachers overlooking the youth parade. Several hundred pounds of explosives had been rigged around the columns upholding the bleachers. At noon they were detonated. One man watching through binoculars as the president waved to the parade had seen his hand fly right off the wrist. "Like a sparrow at the sound of gunshot," he'd later described. One hundred and sixty-three people killed. Probably twice that many detained. It could have been read as a show of incompetence on the son's part, that his security scan of the stadium days prior to the event hadn't turned up a cache of explosives taped to the pylons beneath the bleachers and painted the color of concrete. But the time it would take to formulate such a criticism was quickly filled with a flurry of retributive action. All military-aged males in the village of Kirpukt, the hometown of Sulamir Besmir, the most prominent of the rebel leaders, were detained, brought to Iznek, and subjected to a month of "intensive cross-examination." Tactics of cross-examination had included beatings, sodomization, torture by blowtorch and electrified wires secured to the genitals, followed by execution by pistol, hunting knife, and nail gun. In the words of one observer who had attended the state funeral for Cherkeso the elder, the son had "wept fists" at the service. He'd delivered the eulogy with an announcement of authority, removing a pistol from the shoulder holster beneath his suit, holding it up for the crowd to see, before setting it, with a show of ominous grace, on the podium. This was what the country should expect. Here was a man who protected his interests from a position of deep emotion; and, being a man of the people, his interests were aligned with everyone's.

Anna had to wait eighteen months before she was allowed to contact President the Younger Cherkeso, six more before she was granted council with him. She had spoken by telephone with a series of functionaries, all who claimed to be speaking on behalf of Mr. Cherkeso. Yes, the President had agreed, it was important to develop a relationship with reporters from Moscow. It would be necessary especially in light of the Kremlin's support of his efforts to rebuild and rehabilitate his country's sense of direction and identity. Not seventy years had passed since Stalin's soldiers had marched into Iznek and worked to modernize what was until then essentially a peasant state. They tore down old buildings and built them anew. And when they exhausted the city's supply of stone and brick, they uprooted headstones from the cemeteries and put them to use. This was, the President's representative to the press said, what must be done once again. We must rebuild from the bottom up this country that has, until now, built nothing new but fresh graves.

Anna smiled dryly at that. She had been in country for three months and had seen more than enough fresh graves. The problem was, there weren't enough of them. Public executions had been the chosen deterrent for any rebels still embedded in the villages. In Porguna, forty miles to the west of Iznek, she had witnessed the murder of two men by government security agents. She had stood in the gathering crowd near the oil pipeline outside the village, disguised beneath a burkha, while the two men, possible rebels dressed in track suits, were shot and beheaded. The heads were placed chest-high atop the pipeline. Security agents posed next to them for photos from their camera phones. One of them placed the cigarette between the lips of a dead man then returned it to his own to take a puff. By public order the bodies and heads were not to be buried. They were to be left to rot. "But if the dogs have their way with them," they said, "that will be fine."

She had seen similar things in the south of the country. The president's control was stronger in the east and the north. Moscow had expressed an interest in unifying the country fully by the end of the year. Here it was, halfway through summer, and this deadline seemed all but met. Anna had framed her request to meet President Cherkeso in these terms: to discuss his plans for the country once its regions had been stabilized and local governments had been integrated under his authority. Word was received by her editor in Moscow. Yes, it is time we sat down and outlined in a public manner our plans for the future. The time came sooner than she had thought: "President Cherkeso would be happy to sit down with you later this week, Saturday."

Saturday morning she left her hotel in Iznek early and in a rental car drove west. The President's compound was halfway between the capital and the coastal town of Uzun. The land there was hilly and less populated than along the coast; forests rose and fell like preparatory waves on the way to the sea. Anna kept her notes open on the passenger's seat and listened to the state radio news report, which ended not soon after she had begun listening. A Russian program announcer introduced a symphony by Prokofiev and faintly and slowly the music began, unwinding from a dormant state of dim silence. This was her soundtrack for the trees that rose out of the ground and slowly approached and then, as she reached them, rushed past her. What had Mischa said? To not press the president on his agreement with the Kremlin. To not mention the testimony of exiled rebels. Or the assassinations of defected members of his security force; or the murder of journalists; or the killings of Salim Nazmir in Vienna or Ramzan Yennul in Abu Dhabi. Stay focused on him as a speaker, as a promoter of his own prejudices, as a man in a room. Don't press his answers too forcefully. Pay attention to how convincingly he talks up his plans for reconstituting the government and for rebuilding Iznek especially. We just need a clear sense of how he views himself. How he presents himself will be a large part of that.

Before she had left the hotel that morning, she had told her husband Ilya, "My hands have been shaking for two days now. I want a drink or a Vicodin to calm my nerves." Her husband, also a journalist, had taught her a breathing exercise that he had used in the past; to hold one's arms above one's head and breathe rapidly through the nose; to do this for three minutes and, when done, to hold one's breath for as long as one can and then lay on the floor with eyes closed. He called it his "Five Minute Sanity Session." The tension in Anna's voice was so strong, the cell phone in his hand seemed ready to collapse from the pressure if he let her keep talking; so he asked her to take "five minutes of sanity." "I've already done that, right before I called you," she said. "I know nothing will happen. I'll go there, ask my questions, stir his ire, and then be sent away. He needs to put on a good strong face for the press. Journalists don't have a way of disappearing when they go to talk with him. That comes later. After the articles are published." Ilya could tell she was standing at a window. From the acoustical color of her voice: thinly doubled, with a faint, sharp echo. He was worried for her. This is not where he wanted her to be. Alone, standing in a hotel room, in one of the most ruined cities on the continent, in the world, if one were to draw comparisons.

"Call me any time," he said. "From the drive there. From Cherkeso's place. Remember, we want you back here by the end of the month. We'll coddle you like a batty old heiress. Be safe." She nodded, and then said, "I'm safe. Don't worry. I'm just nervous. More later, Mr. Husband." After they'd said their goodbyes, Ilya sat on the edge of his bed and imagined Anna doing the same, then noted to himself, "You don't get nervous. And now you are." When he looked at the clock on the nightstand, it said nine thirty.

Now that she was driving to meet Cherkeso, her nerves were feeding back into her usual state of calm alertness. What had begun as a quick drive through ugly countryside had gradually become more pleasant. The land between the capital and Uzun was not as ruined as she'd expected. It had rained before dawn, and the dark trees, the small, scattered cottages among them, had a fresh, dewy pastoral loveliness to them. The road shone in patches where the morning light passed through the trees. Due to the humidity there was a sepia quality to the air, miniscule tracers of light refracting by the trillions through airborne specks of water.

She drove without thinking, preparing her instincts for the netting and recording of quick details. This was what she called her "cleaning ritual." Hours before an interview, she would empty her mind of any reference points or opinions of her subject. Not that she was erasing the vital lines leading from the present moment back to the compiled information she had prepared and reviewed weeks beforehand; rather she was clearing the way between the two, so when she needed to draw on some critical particle of data to aid in the formation of a question, the recorded fact would arrive at the right time and from the right angle spontaneously. In the mournfully objective spaces within her was the worst of a country's available history. Ten years of disarray and civil war, revenge killings and government sanctioned executions. These were the generalities afforded by cause and effect: the breaking free of satellite states in the messy twilight months of the Soviet Union, the push for autonomy by tribal leaders against the interests of old loyalists. The civil war of '92-'95, followed by a truce, followed by a second war that began in '97 and continues until now, stalled in a state of perpetual disintegration in this, its last, meanest phase. These were the bare structures of events boiled down to their timelines and held together by a procession of names and dispatches. What was harder to retain were the things seen, the stories relayed to her. These she couldn't affix to a meaningful trajectory.

There was the Muslim woman she had met in Gamurzigol who, having been accused of infidelity against her husband, was arrested by security police and brought to the basement of the police station. There they tied her to an iron pole and beat her with a length of rubber pipe, insisting she confess and beg repentance from her husband. Her husband, of course, was nowhere to be found. Hiding, most likely, at a house in a nearby village.

This was a small, youngish woman with a jagged scab cutting across her upper and bottom lip. She shook and kneaded the back of her neck as she spoke. "I was too afraid to deny it and too afraid to tell them the lie they wanted from me. So I kept quiet."

The police who beat her were young, younger than her, and

laughed and mocked her when she flinched. When they saw that she would admit to nothing, one said with a pious rage that seemed affected, not at all a flourish of righteous feeling, "If you won't confess, you must be punished. You are sentenced to three days of shame." At that they shaved her head and eyebrows with electric shears, then spray-painted the stubble bright green. Pressing her head against the iron pole, one of the officers asked for the can; on her forehead he sprayed an upside down cross beginning at the widow's peak and ending at the bridge of the nose. After this they dragged her into the streets and called bystanders to pelt her with stones and rotten food. She was led to the town square and hand-cuffed her to an old iron ring embedded in the concrete fountain. There she lay for three days, hardly sleeping, begging for food. No one dared look at her, though no one besides the police stopped to mock her.

This was only one of hundreds of stories. Within the neatly memorized pattern of events and official reports existed a chaos of barely verifiable losses, the sheer number of them, as they amassed within her, generated pressure on her conscience, enough, at times, to weaken her composure. There's only so much a conscience can hold and focus into direct action before it collapses inward in a kind of inert, speechless grief. To outmaneuver that grief, which over the past five years had grown more prominent and leaden in her, she had simply written and submitted accounts such as these as quickly as they were relayed to her.

One night, at her hotel in Azran, there was a knock at her door. Outside there a was line of old people. The mothers and fathers of the disappeared in Nalgazalan. One man, a doctor, wept and let the women hold his shoulders as he described his son's abduction six months earlier. "He could not have been anyone to them," he said, "just a bright, happy young man, a computer programmer. Very popular, many friends. There must have been some misunderstanding, he only wanted to keep to himself and raise his family." One morning without notice he was abducted. Armed men wearing masks and camouflage fatigues wrestled him into a black Niva with unnumbered plates. For weeks there was no word of him. His father asked after him at the police station, at the checkpoint outside Nalgazalan. No one he spoke with seemed to know who his son was, where he was held, or why he was taken into custody. On March 5th, twenty-six days after the abduction, the body of a man in his early thirties, badly beaten, hands severed at the wrists, was found face down in a ditch just south of the Nubil Textile factory. The hands were found several paces from the body, sealed in a large clear plastic sandwich bag. This was his son, Amal. Since burying him, he told her, he has not allowed any member of his family to leave the house. If they need food, toys, liquor, words from friends, he would leave on his own and acquire them. This was, she discovered, not an unusual case. Whole neighborhoods in Nagazalan were empty during the late afternoon and evening except for old men running their families' errands.

These, Anna knew, were things she would have to exert discipline against, to repress. Certainly Cherkeso was aware of her dispatches, her articles on Moscow's support of his consolidation of power and terror campaign against communities supportive of the rebels. Since that much was known, that would not need mentioning. She would do as his instructions asked and discuss the answers to the ten questions he selected and would respond to. She would collect evidence of his character and categorize the varieties of justifications for his actions. And most likely he would watch and listen and playfully hint that her removal from the country and his affairs would be very pleasant news to him. For now, she would concentrate on redirecting her fear into intensified tact and alertness.

After an hour, she reached what appeared to be the first of many checkpoints. Three armed men waved her car to the side of the road. After checking her papers, they called her out of her car and walked her across the road to a black UAZ Patrio. She would leave her car there, they said; they would drive the rest of the way. A mile further they arrived at a second checkpoint. More armed men. One more joined them in the back seat, an amiable man wearing a round tyubeteika cap. He laid the assault weapon in his lap so the barrel pointed at an upward angle, toward her chin. For most of the way they sat silently. Passing a number of barracks and guest-houses, they reached the main compound after another half mile. The last checkpoint was flanked on either side by a ten-foot chain link fence. This was topped with layered curls of razor wire. The fence divided the forest in either direction. Beyond this last control post there were three more stops between the gate and the main yard, an hour of inspection and waiting, before the Patrio rolled up the main drive towards a large stone manor house. To Anna's eyes, it looked like a squat, half-sized chalet. At the top of the circular drive, her escorts led her from the jeep through the front entrance, up a wide flight of dark wooden steps, then left past the study to a leisure room in the west wing of the house. In the room sat an array of oversized, dark furniture. A display cabinet filled with ornamental daggers. On the wall opposite the couch and chairs hung a Dagestani rug depicting the deceased Akhmed Cherkeso wearing an astrakhan papkha on his head, against a crimson background. He was portrayed with a forcefully serene expression on his face, eyes narrowed. A sliding glass door opened onto a courtyard. This is where she sat, in the company of several rough, good-humored men and their armaments.

After three hours Gumiel Festarov, director of the largest oil refinery in Lukaev, arrived. The guards stood by mutely. It was then she realized their silence was textured with the contempt of disinterest. When Festarov spoke they looked at each other in agreement. Festarov was a short, springy man in his early forties and as he led her into the courtyard he began describing the upswing in oil production due to the president's actions against the rebels. The majority of the country was secure, the pipelines were pumping thousands of gallons north to Russia each day. "If things stay as they are, or improve," he effused, "we can expect to triple our growth over the next five years."

In the center of the courtyard was a fountain. Of the kind found outside a Spanish villa: classical, decorated with vegetation. Beneath an open terrace, bamboo deck furniture was arranged around a large round glass top table, the price tags still dangling from them. Later Anna would discover this was the house style of decoration; in the bedrooms, in the bathrooms and library, price tags were there if you looked for them. Festarov offered a tour of the house but as he was about to lead her back into the waiting room, the guard with the tyubeteika cap pulled him aside into the hallway. When Festarov returned he said they would have to make do with a short tour of the west wing.

In the guest bedroom her host made it a point of showing her the labels on the dressers, lamps, and mirrors; these, she assumed, were gifts from Festarov himself, "from Hong Kong" he said, with a magisterial pirouette in his voice. No doubt the house was furnished with tributes from tribal leaders, businessmen, families working to protect their interests. In the guest bedroom Festarov stood between two beds, one pink with pink silk sheets, one blue, and lifted both arms in the direction of the flat screen television hung on the wall across from them. In the bathroom, she found tags hanging from the toilet seat, the showerhead, and the mirror. "You should see the Jacuzzi, sauna and swimming pool!" Festarov gushed as he led her back to the waiting room. The flat force of his excitement was familiar. Businessmen who supported Cherkeso often bore themselves with a mix of nervous self-interest and enthusiasm.

At 3:00, with clear relief disguised as graciousness, Festarov excused himself. At 3:30 a bodyguard in a white and gold tracksuit walked in to announce the president would be running late. On the pretense of security he asked that she leave her cell phone with him. Should she need access to a telephone, she was welcome to use the land line, but it was a requirement of all guests to leave their electronics with house security for the duration of their visit. With a direct but discreet tone perfected from years of negotiation, she asked if she might remove the battery from the phone before leaving it with him. After a flat pause, he nodded yes. Since her fingernails were short it took several tries to pry the battery from the phone. After laying it in the man's hand, she dropped the battery into her jacket pocket. It weighed as much as a stone. As he was leaving, she asked him to inquire the staff about the president's list of answers to her prepared questions. "Yes," he replied, "I can tell you. The president does not have time to answer. He will come to talk. Wait here. He will be here soon."

She should have expected this. It was in keeping with what she knew of Cherkeso that he would encourage preparation only to undermine it. One man, an older fighter under Malavna Tvesa during the first war, who had known Cherkeso when he was still on the side of the resistance, described his talent for frustrating expectations. He would work these kinds of disruptions with his friends as much as with his enemies. Once, the old fighter said, he had even encouraged the Russians to hunt him down at the house of a woman he had stayed with. A beautiful, unmannered country girl he had known in grammar school. Every Saturday, if there was no "fire" (rebel slang for an attack or counterattack), he would come down into the village from the forest. Boldly, as if no one knew he wasn't one of Tvesa's fighters. He would walk through the center of town, stop by the barber shop for a shave or haircut, buy a bottle of Struka at the grocery, then head for this woman's cottage. The Russians had informants in the village, he knew this. But for all one day each week he would stay in this woman's cottage as she came and went. And the next morning when he left again for the forest, it was with a rucksack full of foodstuffs and fresh clothes.

For months, he did this. Eventually, after a few skirmishes in the region, the Russians would come through the village several times a week. They threatened the shop owners. They held the barber's fingers over a washing bowl and laid a straight razor to his knuckles. These were things he knew were happening, but every week he walked in an unhurried way into the village. During the week when he was gone, the girl walked quickly to work at the weaver's house, and heading home bore herself with tense silence.

One morning when he was in town the Russians drove into the village. They drove straight to this girl's cottage. They surrounded it and called for him and the girl to come out. They heard the girl call from the cottage. But the door didn't open, so the soldiers shouldered it clear and entered. A half dozen of them were inside when an explosion threw the roof off of it. Bodies were thrown thirty, forty paces. The leg of one man landed on the hood of a Russian armored car. Later people were told that while the girl was about the village doing her errands, Cherkeso had rigged the cottage with explosives armed with a remote detonator. Early in the morning, before dawn, he had woken her, tied her to her bed frame and left. From the forest brush he had watched the Russians surround the cottage and enter. Without any feeling for the girl, he had blown her up along with six men. This was a favorite of Cherkeso, this story, the old fighter under Tvesa said; he told it often.

And now here was another, more formalized variation of that story: Anna, in a chair, in a well-lit, gaudily decorated study, waiting for the protagonist to arrive with his version of the rising action, climax and resolution. She sat in the company of a number of guards who in disorganized shifts came and went. Sometime around six o'clock it began to rain. Not heavily, like the night before, but in loose, leisurely washes of falling water that wandered the grounds outside. On the patio the guards stood together beneath the terrace awning and shared cigarettes. Across from them Anna sat in a square, leather chair facing the sliding door and patio. She opened a pad on her knee, wrote a note, *FSB guards outside,* then flipped to the next page to hide it. The *FSB (Federal Service Bureau)* was the paramilitary arm of the Russian foreign security branch of the military. Cherkeso had come to power with the support of *FSB* operations in the North Caucasus. Since establishing the government he had dissolved a large part of the formal military and built his security force around the *FSB.* This meant he had first say in all local decisions, but the Kremlin had the final word. There was a strong *FSB* presence in Inyulgetma and Abkazia but this was the first instance when a border territory allied with Russian interests established itself as a formal political body with foreign paramilitary support.

As it began to darken outside, she asked one of the men standing near her for the time. It was eight thirty.

The president arrived not long after. Even more armed men arrived with him. On the patio, in the hallway and the study. Stocky, bearded, with a thick crooked nose and small eyes set close together, Cherkeso was dressed in a black windbreaker and black cargo pants. He raised a hand as he sat down at the edge of the couch nearest to her, signaling for her to sit as well. She took his hand as he reached toward hers and shook it, then waited as he unlaced his boots. In socks, he pressed his toes into the carpet until the knuckles cracked. He let out an exaggerated bellow of satisfaction, then rolled his head over to her as if he were finally ready to speak, after several long delays, to someone close to him. "We want to restore order not only in Khruekistan, but throughout the North Caucasus. My people will fight anywhere, even in Russia. But before anything, we must establish stability here, peace. My first directive is to clear the North Caucasus of the older elements. The bandits."

He was beginning mid-conversation. All he had said had been borrowed with little variation from his televised addresses over the past two years. He was a big man and didn't bear himself like an elected official; his body language was still very much a soldier's. As he spoke a threatening energy added momentum to his gestures, as if he were hacking through invisible brush with his hands. It was difficult not to blink excessively when he fought to gain advantage in the conversation, since his hands and his legs were working so actively to expel his thoughts from his body. But this wasn't the case with him alone. While they spoke, his guards also commented on their conversation loudly. Mostly interjections of agreement or, at Anna's expense, suspicion.

"Who do you call bandits?"

"The older fighters. Katrul. Masadov, and others."

"Do you see the mission of your troops as eliminating these men instead of bringing them into detention, rehabilitating them?"

"There is nothing to be done with them," he laughed. "They have been fighting for so long the only thing they know how to do is kill, die, and eat berries. This is a great service for the people, to capture and kill the bandits. They won't allow any kind of order that doesn't involve them." Cherkeso gestured to one of the men for a beer. Another man near the doorway to the adjoining room turned on a television in the corner and left it on mute.

"Well, why not involve them? It seems everything done in the name of unification until now has involved killing and liquidating.

In interests of unifying the country wouldn't it be best to extend amnesty to the rebels?"

"This is already happening. Eight hundred people have already surrendered to us and are living a normal life. And when they come back to their families and see what they've done, having abandoned them for so long, this is a good thing. What the bandits must know is the resistance doesn't just affect them. It has taken fathers and sons from their families. It is time for them to come home and act like men, support their elders, wives and children. The people want to put the war behind them. That is what the majority wants. A great majority!" At this Cherkeso spread his arms widely before him. The man he had sent for the beer stepped forward and placed the beer in his outstretched hand. Cherkeso nodded pragmatically, smiled, and then sipped the beer. Some of the other men in the room were drinking as well.

"Do you believe Katrul will surrender? He is much older than you. It would be unusual if he did so."

"It does not matter. It would be better to take him alive. Then the people could see how old and tired he is. We would keep him in a cage, put him on live television, surely! So they could see."

"It has been said people in the south still support him."

"They are misled. I have spoken with the women in these villages. They have come to me, they have pleaded with me, 'Sulim, Katrul has stolen our sons into the forest. He has promised them money if they join him in the forests, but there is no money and he keeps them there without a choice to come home. Sulim, bring our sons back, bring death to this bandit!' These boys do not know they are fighting for the wrong side. It's our job to show them where the future is, to leave the forests and help us rebuild, instead of pulling all of us back into the Cave Age! Anyway, Katrul is not a problem. Eventually we will find him. He is of little concern."

"And Masadov?"

"Masadov is different. Masadov is a warrior."

"It seems that, where you are dismissive of Katrul, you have real respect for Masadov."

"He is not a coward. He is a fighter. What I would like is to meet him in open battle, with no outside influences, just his men and my men in direct fighting, no hiding. Then it would be decided who is the better fighter."

"And what if Masadov won?"

"Impossible! I never lose. Anyway, I do not consider Masadov an enemy. An opponent merely."

"What is the difference?"

"An enemy is someone who wants what you have and tries to take it by indirect means. An opponent is someone who wants nothing from you, and who respects you enough to attack you directly. Katrul is an enemy, certainly. He would like nothing more than to have the Kremlin's support, these men behind him. He hides in the forests and attacks at night, never in numbers larger than ten or twenty. Masadov despises the Russians, despises Katrul and everyone else. He fights in large numbers, to the death, by daylight. And when he strikes where there are civilians, he shows no mercy."

"And that is something to respect?"

"Certainly. It is not easy to be a leader. Masadov is a leader. He does not let feelings for others get in the way of decisions. I can admire him, but being an elected leader I cannot be that way. My feeling for the people and my demand for order are equal," he said, holding his open hand flat at eye level. "Even."

Cherkeso began to unzip his windbreaker. Beneath it he wore a tie and crisp navy blue dress shirt. Setting his beer on a side table he stood, removed the windbreaker and handed it to one of his men then drew the elastic waistline of his cargo pants to his ankles. A pair of gray slacks was beneath them. He adjusted the knot on his burgundy tie, smoothed it down its length then took his seat again with an air of bemusement.

"Enough of Masadov. Next question."

"Just one more. Six months ago your men captured Masadov's bodyguard Kalseh Adaman Ulin. Where is he now?"

A smile. "We have him under house arrest not far from here. We could bring him here, if you like. You could speak with him, no inconvenience. We use him for negotiations. The rebels know him. He has been very useful and cooperative."

"Not long ago on television he called himself a traitor."

"Not so, he did not say this and he is not a traitor. He is a responsible countryman. He surrendered out of good conscience, as he said. Not true that we captured him."

"His leg was amputated. He had been injured while fighting?"

"Yes, but he had been injured long before he surrendered. Such are the conditions in which these rebels live. They can't even take care of their own! Anyway, I have him not far from here. I could have him brought here within minutes."

"That is okay, I wouldn't want to wake him."

"Nonsense. He would be happy to come." The men around

the room laughed and looked at her. Cherkeso, though, watched her hand as it jotted notes on the pad open on her thigh. Once it stopped moving, he nodded at it, "Note finished. What else?"

"What are your strengths and weaknesses?

"What? I don't understand."

"What are your weaknesses as a person, as a leader?"

"I have none."

"And your strengths?"

At this, without smiling, he opened his hands and gestured to the room around them. After a short pause he translated the gesture into words: "Strengths speak for themselves. Besides," he added, "busy men don't have time to think about strengths and weaknesses. They act. Only the weak have time to think about such things."

Looking at Cherkeso, Anna remembered a press photo she had once seen of him. Either the color of his tie or the beer in his hand had reminded her: of the newly appointed president standing before reporters at a private dinner, his cabinet and foreign investors around the banquet table, a golden revolver, a gift from Yeshtriko, CEO of Zukkor Mining, in his right hand, and in his left a microphone held inches from his mouth. When she had first seen it the photograph had struck her as crass; but when at parties or in discussions with friends or other reporters it came to mind as she described the character of the man. But now she thought of that other element of the photograph, the gold-framed portrait of the Russian Prime Minister hanging on the wall behind him, over his left shoulder. Between the microphone and his mouth, the corner of the gilded frame angled perfectly, as if arranged by design instead of by whim of the frozen moment. This she hadn't noticed before: the gold of the portrait frame and the revolver afforded a perfect symmetry. And this, more than the revolver itself, might have been the reason the photograph asserted a stronger pull on her memory.

And now here he was, Cherkeso explaining himself, declaiming.

"The Kremlin and the Prime Minister have given us their full support. Just as well as us they want to see Khruekistan united. The Prime Minister has offered access and command over any resources we need, but I told him, 'No, this is our country, our mess to put right.' But if needed, I could call him any time of day and have two battalions under my command, no questions."

"Has there ever been an instance when there had been need for military assistance?"

"Never. And there won't be. The only assistance we need is with keeping certain people from our business."

"Which people?"

"You."

Cold waves of tension made their way down Anna's legs to her ankles. "Who do you mean by 'you'?"

"Journalists, people like you. Politicians. You don't let us sort things out. You divide us. You come between Khruekistanis. You personally are the enemy. You are worse than Masadov."

"When peace is established, and the country has been rebuilt, will there be elections?"

"Of course. A six-year cycle. But only once the government is established."

"Will you run during that first election?"

"I have already run once, so no."

"There was an election?"

"Yes, I was voted into office two years ago, by members of parliament. Elected representatives of the people."

"So you will not run again for the first direct election."

"I will not. I will retire."

Anna placed the cap back onto the pen, slid it into the spiral binding of her notepad. She had followed his answers too far into the kind of questions Michsa had advised against. Mischa and Ilya, and the photographer Rikorski, who had spoken with Cherkeso once at a policy dinner. "With him, keep all serious questions under the spell of pleasantries," he had said. "His answers will show soon in the next news cycle."

"And what will you do then?"

"I will take up bee farming. Already I have bees, and bullocks, and fighting dogs."

"Fighting dogs? Don't you feel sorry when they kill each other?"

"Not at all. I respect them. I respect my dog Napoleon as much as any man. He's a Caucasian sheepdog. Those are the most fair-minded dogs there are."

On the television near the adjoining doorway the Russian Prime Minister was speaking. The volume was muted and several guards were talking over the images of reporters and the Prime Minister.

"Now there is a man," Cherkeso said, pointing at the screen. "Very intelligent." After a few seconds of footage of the Prime Minister walking to his car, he added, "See there, how he walks? I had always wondered, even after the first time we met, he reminded me of something. He walks like a mountain dweller! I even told him so."

After several minutes a group of men came to the sliding glass door. Two helped another other step into the study from the patio. It was Kalseh Adaman Ulin. "The Pride of the Nation," "The Hero of the Nation," a graying man of thirty-two. The guards led him to a large wooden chair that had been pulled from a corner to the center of the room. Not until he took this seat did the guards remove their hands from his armpits. Another man, older, thin, with a full unkempt beard, stood to the right of Ulin. Though he did not rest his hand on the back of the chair, it seemed that at any moment he would. This was the interpreter. Ulin, Cherkeso explained, did not speak Russian fluently, though from the keenness with which Ulin followed their conversation Anna doubted this.

"This is a reporter. From Russia," the president said with the same brisk control he addressed Anna with. "She has asked about Masadov. I have told her that you surrender to us after fighting with him. Tell her, so there will no more questions about that: you surrendered."

The interpreter spoke to Ulin but Ulin did not look up. With both hands flat on his left thigh, he watched the carpet with a dignified blankness. Neither nodding nor shaking his head, he looked at them, from the president to Anna, from Anna to Cherkeso, and replied with a few short words. The interpreter translated Ulin's response into several sentences about Masadov's lack of provisions, his inability to properly treat the wounded, about Ulin's leg injury and Masadov's indifference to it. "I surrendered," the interpreter said, "Not just to get treatment, but because it was clear Masadov's care for all Khruekistanis would be as good for others as it had been for me."

As the interpreter spoke Ulin continued to stare at the carpet.

"That's it," Cherkeso said, turning to everyone in the room. "See? That's all we needed to hear. Tell him 'thank you' and that he can go now."

Ulin looked over his shoulder before the interpreter could tap the chair. While Ulin rose two men stepped to help him up.

Anna stood as well, but Ulin didn't look at her. There was a brief moment as the guards helped him through the door. His shoulder had caught the doorframe on his way onto the patio, or his foot had slipped on the wet metal sliding track; but the grip of the men tightened and helped him up. When the door slid shut behind them, Cherkeso stood as well. Turning to her he said, "A good meeting. It's late though. Now you must be going as well."

The phrasing, the slight lift in which it was delivered, was precise enough to tighten the muscles in her stomach.

"Come back in a year or so, when we have really begun to straighten things out."

In a short, almost calibrated series of actions, he shook her hand, led her to the hallway where the drivers were waiting. The drivers led her out of the west wing to the main foyer, down the main staircase, through the front door and into the Patrio idling on the drive. Not until they had curled around the drive and down the hill through the manor gate did she remember the phone she had left with house security. She asked the men in the front seat to turn around. The front passenger, the man in the tyubeteika cap, adjusted the rear view mirror to answer, his mouth turned away from her while his eyes held hers directly. "Not now. We will have it sent later to your hotel. Tomorrow morning you can pick it up at the front desk."

When they reached the first control post, two men stepped from the car. As they reached the next stop, the other guard reached to clap the driver on the shoulder and left. For the rest of the drive Anna sat in the middle of the back seat as the driver steered into the light cast by the headlights on the road. There was no one on the road. As they approached the checkpoints, men strode into the headlights and waved them past. A weak weight began to harden between her eyes, between her breasts, gathered density in her stomach, and after several attempts, in as even a voice she could shape from her throat, she asked the driver: "Are you driving me to my car?"

The driver didn't turn and kept steering, so in a quieter voice she asked again.

"Yes," the driver responded. He spoke with a southern accent.

"Don't worry. And don't cry," he said. Though she hadn't made a sound and he hadn't looked in the mirror to see her, it was true, she was crying.

"You are strong," he said. And then: "That won't happen."

ATOWN

And isn't this the place—the town—you'd heard about? Aren't these the trees, the hills of pounded, dirty grass? Those people a few hundred yards away, aren't they townspeople? This must be a town, because those are certainly townspeople, exhausted, thin, living off the scraps the rest of us, the bystanders, outsiders, have tossed to them.

And is it a town if you can't leave? If you can enter, yes, it's a town. But what if you didn't know you had entered it? What if, one day, you are walking or riding your bike or driving west from some of other town, or southeast of Penn's Branch, which isn't a town, but a favorite camping place for city folk who leave to spend a weekend under the stars awash in the hiss of cicadas, and unbeknownst to you, you cross into this place and notice these people, these castaways from other towns, crouching in the shadows of their makeshift huts? What then? Do you stop, do you talk to them? Do you ask them, what is this place? This is in the middle of farm country, there's not a slum within a hundred miles. What would so many people be doing here, strewn about in such an unkempt condition? No camping gear, no electricity or running water?

But if there is a stream nearby, couldn't it be said they have access to running water? And if from the remains of the belongings they have brought there they happen to fashion blankets, walls, roofs, buckets, knives and spears, couldn't it be said they have gear to aid in their survival?

When you leave your car, will you be afraid? Will you carry a map with you, but also a serrated hunting knife sheathed in your belt? Will they stare at you? Will they gather in groups of five and seven and three and discuss among themselves the fact of your presence? Or will they even care, will they even register your approach with anything other than disinterest?

Now that you're standing among them, women, men and children, what will you ask them? Will you ask, What is this place? Will you turn to an older woman, squinting as if she'd lost her glasses, and ask, Where do you hail from? Or to all of them, the gaunt, the barelegged and sunburned, will you ask, How long has this place existed, how long have you been here?

It's a town, they'll say, it's been here longer than anyone, and if you hadn't arrived here, driving west on a road you had spied on the map, a shortcut between interstates, you would have said to them, that's no answer at all. But who's to say what constitutes a town? Somewhere between the intimacy of villages and the expansiveness of cities, a town has always occupied a tenuous place in the advance of civilizations upon the wilderness. Who's to say when a village becomes a town, or a town a city? Who's to say if towns exist at all?

It's a town, they will tell you, and we came our own way, one or two or four at a time. When they explain who they are and where you are, will you look around you? Will you watch their faces and then follow their line of sight? And if you do, what will you see? Will you see others just like them, veritable townspeople, standing alone or striding along some undefined perimeter? Will you ask the old woman and the burned man with the mustache and bony arms, What are they doing, those people over there? Oh, they're watching for any newcomers, they'll say, then with hard irony, Like you. To which the mustache man will add: some may be trying to work up the nerve to step out and scorch themselves.

And what will that mean? To step out, to scorch themselves? What will that man, stroking his mustache, a flick of Johnson grass dangling between his teeth, have just told you? That they plan to light themselves on fire? That these burns, abrasions, scorch marks on the arms, cheeks, backs, kneecaps, torsos of the townspeople around you are intentional?

And won't it seem that, before the man had mentioned this, you hadn't noticed them, the wounds in various states of healing covering their bodies? When you ask them why, won't they laugh, one or two or a dozen or so who squat or sit within earshot? Won't they laugh in that flat manner of the initiated bearing down on the obtuseness of the innocent?

See the ground, they'll ask. Notice how tramped down it is? Now look yonder, what do you notice? When you follow the point of their finger, across the tramped ground, you see grass growing in spare sprigs here and there until, farther away, it begins to push up again and even farther out, flourish.

Will you notice the ditches running along the road doing the same? Beaten earth gradually coming up green as it stretches off into the distance, the precise distance from which you came?

Will you understand then? Will it be clear? Will you hear them tell you what it means to be in a town, or in this place at least? Will they tell you in as much detail as they can offer, drawing on their limited abilities of description, that anyone who steps beyond a certain point will fall painlessly into a puddle of viscera and wet ash? Those are the town limits. Expect a quick death if you step beyond them. Dozens better than you have tried. Will you believe them then, when they tell you? Or better put, will there be anything to gain from doubting them?

Will you hear the old woman then tell you the town's history, which is a history of people coming and not going, arriving and not leaving, as if coming and arriving were the same thing—coming, as if they were drawn there, arriving, as if they had always intended to come? How some people have been here for five, ten years, sometimes more, and often, out of cabin fever or boredom, rush past the town limits to their own quick end? And won't that also be an integral part, perhaps the most poignant part, of a town's history? The grass around it is very green, and those are the town limits? But also, quite literally, the town's cemetery?

Every day more people join the others and walk the edges, and in a perfect circle they take their shadows for a walk, sometimes casting them on the packed dirt of the town, sometimes on the healthy grass of its cemetery, depending from what angle the sun chooses to shine down on them. Won't they be doing the same even now? Won't that be what you're seeing? Watching those people on the edge, will it make you nervous, will you want to call out to them?

Down the road, a car wavers out of a heat cloud. Where did it come from? Did it come from where you came? How will it be received? Will dozens of people drop what they're doing and come running? Will some stand along the road's edge waving the car on? Will others jump and shriek "No"? Will others squat in groups of three or four to throw loose money on the ground? Won't the mustache man's mustache disappear beneath his cupped fingers as he blows on a slim length of grass? Won't he tell you what you can already guess, since you've been here long enough to know how a town holds its council? Won't he say, This is how some choose to pass their time, betting who will enter and who will stop cold and turn around?

And won't you remember your own approach then, and won't you blame yourself? Your thoughtless fiddling with the car stereo? Your missing the cues entirely, those people waving you on, those others yelling no?

The car slows as it crests the last hill. It stops, it turns around. It leaves as if it knew what it was driving towards.

And what will you feel then? Relief, disappointment? Resentment? Or will it be an easy mixture of all three, which you erase quite naturally, wiping your hands down your face?

The people along the road come down all together in a crowd, talking without turning to each other. Some have money in their hands, others walk back with empty pockets, knowing tomorrow they'll have a chance to earn back their losses. But when they run out of money, what then?

It will be dark in an hour. Then it will be dark. After a few hours, someone will say in a few hours it will be lighter. So goes the days and nights in a small town.

And how should this settle with the people living there? The narrower the town limits, the faster they seem to shrink. Will huts in the old part of town gradually be abandoned? Will new ones be built on top of each other and gradually, because word has gotten around to citizens of nearby towns, will a crowd begin to gather on the outskirts? Soon there are hundreds of people standing there, some with camera phones, hand-held recorders, others with microphones; some with bags of food bought in bulk; some with floodlights, others with penlights, most with headlights projecting from the grills of their cars. Will long-estranged family members, girlfriends, husbands, children of townspeople be among them? Will your daughter, Lucy Ann, stand on the hood of a truck and wave? And when you wave back, will you at last count yourself as one of them, a person who so happens to live in a town?

And how long will that take? How long will any of it last? How small will the town grow, plowing through the crowd of people pushed together in a bundle at its center? Will there be a smell? The sizzle of flesh and bone, parts of people to the front and back of you, an arm here, a foot there, a nose right down to the sinuses? Will the weeping and hot press of people against each other and the surprised shouts and pleas for help from people watching outside the town quiet down, as the limits shrink to hold only one or two or three people, then one or two, and then one, then barely one, the final person, the last left standing with shoulders hunched, eyes wide, a skirt of wet ash stretching fifty feet on the ground all around and away from him?

And will he be you? Will he have any last words to convey to the citizens of neighboring towns gathered around him? Will he say, As mayor, I hereby return the rights of this charter to the people of Penn's Branch, Williamsborough, Brookington, Crow Path, Paint Bank, Collinswood, Acton, Pushville, Pallsville, and Nitro. And moreover, do transfer rights of these trees, this ground, that stream, road, field of grass to the people of said commonwealths? May they value them. May they use them well. And when he says this, when he makes this commitment, this promise, this pledge, will it be final? And if not, how will you know?

A THING ABOUT MOUTHS

The things people will do, to regain their mouths. Easy enough to remember how they lose them. Short on funds, they resolve to not eat for a day, then one day turns into another, and soon their mouths harden and dry up. Or someone they owe money to punches them, knocks the mouth right off them. Or their sweetheart gets angry about something, and to exorcise the ill mood, slaps them hard right on the mouth. When they pull their hand away, there it is, squashed right there and squirming in the palm of their hand.

I've heard worse cases. Once, John Lee Cane, this friend of a friend, was so hard up for cash he actually sold his mouth to a mouth dealer; this was in central Florida, at one of those huge flea markets where they sell everything under the sun—live shrimp, doll houses, prosthetic limbs, puppies. He didn't have any valuables to hock, but he met a guy, and this guy led him to a back room behind an indoor chain link fence, and between them they cut a deal to buy his mouth for two hundred fifty dollars. It was enough to clear that month's rent, and he thought, when I can scrape together some seasonal work, I'll buy it back, at a markup price, sure, but still. He was a tree doctor. It was a few weeks from the stormy season. He usually counted on a few busy weeks to make up for the lean months during the winter; but this year, the storms didn't come, the skies were placid as a glass of milk, and eventually they had to sell his mouth via internet auction to an old woman in Texarkana. He tried to plead his case, but that's no easy task without a mouth. With the money that eventually did come in, he paid for adult education courses in sign language.

Hard times. This other friend of mine, Laurie, for the sake of anonymity call her Laurie X, had a job for a while storing and cleaning these things—worked for a buyer and seller of mouths. There was a small warehouse in Northwest Jersey filled with them, they kept them in jars preserved in some kind of special solution, saline or something, and it was her job to catalogue incoming and outgoing shipments. This place was a hub for the international mouth market, she thought, and most of the mailing lists were to addresses in Russia and Western Europe. But the incoming shipments were from all over the place—China, Kazakhstan, Indonesia, Brazil, but of course the old skittishness about race still held true for mouths, not many from Africa. Her boss, one of those shady New York types, said Africa was the future. There're more healthy mouths in Africa than on any other continent, and people would be happy to sell them off for next to nothing. There was a packing facility and a scrappy looking laboratory in an outbuilding on the far end of the storage park, but she didn't see how they handled the mouths once they unpacked them. All she did was print out

EAN-13 barcodes and tape them to the jars then number them on the bottom with a marker. They all looked roughly the same, really. Like half-molded sculptures of gelatin, sometimes with teeth showing, often not, and if she rotated the jar enough and angled it in the light just right she'd eventually find the lips caught in some lost, mummified expression. She didn't last long. It crept her out, sitting in a warehouse six days a week surrounded by other people's mouths. It made her think of all the mouthless people out there, drinking through their noses, living by stomach feed through shunts in their bellies. Her last day, she bought a mouth, searched the home address of the person who had sold it, and mailed it back express. You'd have better luck going out to some wild spot and setting it free, her boss said. He knew it'd be back across his desk within a week.

Not that I'd judge his sarcasm. I have much of it myself. It's hard not to sniff some personal motive stinking up some do-gooder's sweet gestures—but still, a guy has to keep his hopes up, even if something horrible gets beneath it, and props it up eye level.

Take the case of my aunt Astrid. My uncle Gree heads north again one winter, like he always does, to work in the mines way up in Canada. A month later word comes back from the foreman: my uncle has been crushed by a crane spade, a freak accident. Astrid asks to have the body sent back. They write back, the body's in no condition to be sent. She says, send it anyway, in separate storage containers if you have to. They say, can't do. His contract stipulated that in event of fatal trauma on the worksite, his bodily organs should be donated to the company hospital. Included in the list of organs was her favorite part of him: his mouth. Such a classic, movie star mouth. A manly pout. Like early Brando, or Pacino. The kind of mouth that betrayed a fickle mix of free-range sensuality and woundedness. She was wildly angry at that, my aunt, that they would confiscate his mouth. That they could do that. After threats of litigation, they even sent her photographs of it, to prove that it did in fact still exist and was in fact intact, a living, familiar part of him. I was there when she opened the envelope. I saw her. She spread the 8x10 glossy photo on the counter and held it down on either side with both hands, stared long and deep at it until her body started shaking in that ugly, involuntary way that's awkward to listen to and look at. She pinned it up by her bed. She said goodnight to it. Months later I came by and saw a second framed photograph next to it. Her mouth, she told me, she'd gone to a professional studio and had it taken, the rest of her face photoshopped out. Now what is a person supposed to do about that? I let it be. I crouched eye level to both on their respective nightstands and looked at them a respectful amount of time, and then went back to the kitchen to unbag the groceries I had bought. Who's to judge? I did a few things for her when she needed it, and usually didn't think enough about it to wonder why; she had her sons, though, and her daughter Lucy, and yet there I was every week or so, coming by to do little favors. It was when she started closing the door to the bedroom when I came by that I understood why: if I didn't get to take at least one quick peek in there, to gauge the look of that room, I'd leave with a feeling of disappointment.

I'm an okay guy, I'm sure anyone would tell you, but what can I say—I'm not perfect. A better listener than a talker, for sure. It's this business about the mouths that leaves me wary of people. What they'll do to get rid of them. What they'll do to get them back. It's almost as if they hock them off for the trouble of finding a way to buy them back. I might have to try it someday. Though I have this mouth, and I'm talking, maybe that's not the point. Maybe I'm missing something.

LOST DANCES

1) **Ballet With Phantom Limbs**. (1975). *Paige Hamid*. An ampu-
tee ballet. Hamid's notes specify the dancers should be veterans of
the most recent war. The piece a scene by scene recreation of *La
Bayadere*, or, if the budget allows, *The Nutcracker*, with wheelchairs,
crutches, and amplified noisemakers. At the completion of the
ballet prosthetic limbs are thrown at the bowing cast, like roses.

2) **The Six Mary Vinas**. (1959). *Oscar Lutz*. A set piece to be performed outdoors in urban environments. Props: one piece of chalk,
six homeless women, two hundred one dollar bills, a ladder. The
set: on a street or sidewalk. In chalk draw six smallish circles equi-
distant from each other. Ten paces away draw one 10X10 square.
Instruct the women (the six "Mary Vinas") to each choose a circle
to stand in. When the piece begins, the women are to fall on their
hands and knees and lick the chalk of their circles. The first one
finished is the first to run to the square, where money is already
fluttering down from the height where the director stands, atop

his ladder. Once the square is filled with all six Marys, throw the money by fistfuls, watch them fight for it like carp over pinches of bread. Once all of it has been pocketed, the crowd steps forward with straw brooms. Together they sweep away the edges of the square. The Marys walk away, all the richer.

3) **Ode to Linus Pauling**. (1997). *Angela Ignacio Reval.* Of course the piece bears no discernible relation to Pauling, two-time Nobel laureate, whose research explored the structure of chemical bonds. Reval's first specification: the piece is only to be performed in Chicago. Six dancers, one for each El line. Red, blue, brown, orange, green, purple. Starting at the stop furthest from downtown, and beginning in the rearmost car of the train, dancers repeat certain actions in each car for five minutes until they reach the front. Once they reach the front car, they repeat these actions in reverse, five minutes per car, back where they came from. Once the trains reach the Loop, each dancer sings a song of their own making. Jolly, sad, no matter. When the trains reach Clark & Lake, at the Thompson Center, they set off, follow the crowd. In the main plaza the dancers take their bow. Applause from the audience, confused or not, is welcome.

4) **Foot Vox**. (2003). *Groupa Etna.* Technically, a "ballet of dirt." Several floor fans are positioned around a large room. The room's walls are lined with aluminum bleachers, where the audience is invited to sit. A dance in three acts: Low, Medium, & High, according to the settings of the fans. Begins at "Low," dirt skitters across the floor. At "Medium" dust begins to billow. At "High" the room

is fully clouded. The audience is invited to wear goggles and dust masks issued to them in the lobby. Five minutes into "High" two tall men dressed in burlap overalls shuffle into view carrying feed shovels. Scoop, toss into the air, dance into the drop of it which plumes up as smoke. After ten minutes they lean the shovels against each other in the middle of the room and, back to back, walk away. The fans are unplugged. The men lay down. The piece: settled.

5) **Non Finito (For Rosa)**. (1964). *Rosa Smith*. Composed for self-performance. Lights rise on one woman, naked, holding a white long-stemmed rose, staring at it with supreme concentration. Willing it to grow. Boos from the audience are integral.

6) **A Suicide For Paula Glade**. (1977). *Norma McHollis*. An interesting history. Preparation for this piece was extensive. McHollis translated the English alphabet into a vocabulary of small gestures and movements (ie. "m" was denoted by a sharp lowering of the chin, "x" by a splaying of fingers of one's right hand). This catalog of gestures bore many variations and depended on a number of subtle valences. For example, lowercase "f" was represented by a crossing of arms across one's chest, while capital "F" required that one hug oneself violently. With this catalog of movements McHollis translates the diary entry of a fourteen year old girl, dated July 12, 1963, detailing her rape by a friend of her mother's. The girl killed herself before the diary was found. McHollis "rewrites" this confession into a solo piece. Spaces between words are represented by ten second intervals of stillness. The end of each sentence is marked by a thirty second interval. The piece concludes with the dancer

standing stock still, expressionless, for an hour. Sometimes longer.

7) **Meat Joy II**. (1969). *The Cut Collective*. Post-Actionist psycho-drama/improvisation. Within a 7X10 cage, prosthetic limbs slick with pigs' blood are thrown onto a trampoline. Several animals are set loose: pigs, chickens. Recordings of circular saws are played at high volume. Men in red robes surround the cage on all sides and chant, in grunting intonations, "Schnee-mann... Schnee-mann." During which Carolee Schneemann is called on speaker phone to comment.

8) **Tête-à-Tête**. (1971). *Ben Fuller*. One minute piece. Two women in headstand positions relate their worst fears to each other in monosyllabic sentences.

9) **If There Were Even More Than A Thousand Fewer People You Know I Would Still Stoop To Help Them Up Over The Lone Ridge**. (1957). *Heavenlanders*. A Western. Men in men's clothing and women in women's clothing. A tautological study of gender. But wait—the men have long hair, women have short. Women, though, are taller than the men. They knock each other over then help one another up. Seemingly unstructured but as the program notes relate, this is the first and only piece created according to a visual modification of the 12-tone technique, extrapolated from Schoenberg's system for serial composition. All collisions are calculated; all extended hands, specified.

10) **I Love Piano**. (1993). *Alanna Valencia*. Man masturbates onto

the keys of a piano then sits down to play "While My Lady Sleeps."

11) **Boredom Bit**. (1999). *Dick Higgins.* Composed post-mortem, after Higgins' death. Computer generated series of set movements, calculated according to the height, weight, and age of Dancer #1. Nearby, Dancer #2 kneels off-stage. Dancer 2 rolls pennies across the stage, towards Dancer 1. Once ten dollars' worth of pennies has been rolled, the piece is announced to be over. For an encore, pennies are swept off the stage into the audience.

THE SMOKE LEPER

"Have you ever seen one, Myoko?" Mr. Naguchi asked, "A smoke leper?"

I shook my head. The lines on his face caught the candle-light from the paper lanterns, creased it into a sharp mesh of black cuts and shadows. The only other face I had seen like this was the mummy of a young girl the lake fishermen had dredged from the gas shallows, ten, twenty years ago.

"They were talked about much more when I was younger. When I was a boy, my *Nit-Nit* (grandmother) would tell stories about the valley between Oze and Endra Mountains, three valleys over from where your Uncle Tamura planted his apple orchard. It was filled with 'untethered spirits,' as they called them, 'moon be-ings'—smoke lepers."

Mr. Naguchi bit a dried apple chip and lightly patted the sugar dust from his hands. I was poking the fire with a birch limb. Spirals of hot embers spun in an updraft of night cold and fire. I had found the limb while walking the short way to his hut, along the cliff line, sticking straight out of the earth where it had fallen. Mr. Naguchi reached to stop my hand and catch my eye.

"They were once good men, like me or you, and now they are vapors, like steam curling off morning tea. They frighten passersby, but have no understanding—where the passersby come from, why they are afraid. Of all the demons of the earth, they are most like us, confused. Once, when I was younger, half the age you are now, my mother got sick with fever, and my father brought me to stay at my Uncle Tamura's for the summer and third season. I helped him tend the apple trees, and, when it was time for harvest, helped pick them. We filled basket after wicker basket, and often, in the high weeks of harvest, rose an hour, two hours before dawn. If the dew dried too quickly on a slightly nicked apple, my uncle believed it would spoil the whole fruit.

"My mother was ill all through the summer and into the third month, so I stayed, often worrying about her, though these worries were strangely detached—I couldn't remember what she looked like, when she was healthy. Only as I last saw her, before my father had carried her by horseback to the sanitarium. Small, pale, like a worm's dream of a woman. So when I woke early in the morning, to the sounds of my uncle banging dried clods from his boots, it was with this alien face in mind—my mother's, ill-white, hollowed, dull.

"It must have been in the second week of morning harvests when we noticed some of the apples were eaten. Some bore the marks of adult teeth on them, some had large chunks bitten from them. More than a few were perfectly skeletonized, so to speak, chewed down to the core and clinging by their stems, like little hourglasses, their meat just beginning to brown. *'Lukis'*, my uncle said, 'moon beings, smoke lepers.'

"I had heard of them, but never believed in such a thing, earth spirits. My father, a self-taught but scholarly man, had frequently dismissed talk of the dead and the visitation of ancestors as the fantasies of fearful, unscrupulous minds. But my uncle, having never left his valley, was more aware of what came and went, and left its mark in quiet ways, as a warning.

"'*Rada* (nephew),' he said, 'tonight we will set our traps and wait for them.' I did not understand, so he took me to his cottage and rolled away the large rug in the middle of its floor, and opened the trapdoor that had been hidden there. Stacked in neat rows: dozens of large, shallow, wide-brimmed clay bowls. He held one to my eyes and turned it so I could see from every angle. 'These will do,' he said, and we carried them into the orchard. Beneath each tree, on a pile of stones, we laid a bowl, and filled each, not with water, as I had thought, but with a month's worth of milk from his kennel goats. By evening, he led me on his rounds to inspect them—three, four dozen bowls filled to the brim with level milk, the leaves, trunks and branches reflected in miniature and still as the mountains themselves. After picking a few gnats from them, we walked to the cottage and climbed in bed and slept. Before the chill had left my feet, my uncle was snoring. And the noise of his breathing, and my fear, like a letter-knife between the eyes, kept me awake. But I heard nothing all night long.

"An hour before dawn, my uncle's snoring stopped, and a moment later he sat up. '*Rishi* (boy), wake up. Work to do.' But I was already up, holding my socks but waiting for him to pull his own on. I was trembling, thinking of the apples, the bowls, and, briefly, of an old woman, sitting up, holding the hands of a much younger woman to her face, turning them before her, to inspect them. It was my mother, I realized, as I couldn't see her, as I imagined her, and no sooner had I thought this, my uncle handed me a hoe and, pitchfork in hand, ducked out the door.

"The night was crisp, clear, and the ground was cold. You could see the stars, the outlines of the mountains, black where the stars ended. The trees stood all around us just as we had left them, his cottage in the middle of a valley in the shape of a nearly perfect circle. There were thin, bright glints scattered beneath the trees, and these, I realized, as we walked toward one, were the bowls we had arranged the evening before.

"My uncle approached one without timidity, fear or nervousness. He bent over it naturally, brushed dust from its rim, looked up at the tree, reached for an apple, inspected it. I circled the bowl, though, resting on its small pile of stones four paces from the trunk of a twisted, stunted, thick-branched tree. The earth was dark around it, the bowl too; but the milk itself, strangely white—like moonlight, and undisturbed, and, I noticed, leaning over it, placid, blank, unbothered by any reflection.

"'It's in there,' my uncle said, tapping the side of the bowl with his finger. '*A Luki.*' When he tapped the bowl again, I noticed—no movement, no ripples. 'Come, let's gather them up. Walk softly, make sure not to spill a drop.' By dawn we had carried most of them to the dirt yard by the cottage, and as my uncle instructed, laid them in eight straight rows of six on the ground. They glowed there and looked like giant, submerged pearls seen from up high, from a cliff. All that morning, my uncle and I sat on the stone rim of his well and watched as they dried and did nothing. By evening, they had evaporated a little, the milk a quarter of an inch lower. Next morning we rose and did the same. And the morning after.

"Days later the last of the pale white milk was gone. 'Dry as the mouth of a beggar,' my uncle said, 'Gone for good.' That month, he said after we had finished, was the best harvest in years. After we had tied the apple crop in their hutches, we gathered the bowls as well, stacked them carefully in even numbers, and placed them in their box beneath the ground. The first week of winter, my father arrived on horseback with the good news: my mother, though still weak, was healthy, and home again.

"This I can still remember very clearly: when she lifted me up into her lap later that day, I was astonished at how soft my mother's cheek was, when I touched it."

LAST MAN

Friends last longer than first loves but it's not always true they leave a deeper impression. Except the ones who come to a bad end. Those stick with you a while. They lead the way, you could say. My friend Steve, my Friday night drink for three years when I lived in Baton Rouge, damaged his liver but in a show of manliness ignored it. When I saw him last his skin had turned yellow and the whites of his eyes were pink as a rabbit's. He was still talking about moving north, where supposedly some more dignified form of employment awaited him. He cleaned the toilets of St. Aloysius' Elementary. A job fit for a man who couldn't stop laughing at the bottomless debasements available to a person with no money or prospects. King Oliver, he told me, possibly the greatest jazz man before Louis Armstrong left New Orleans, died a janitor in a small town in Georgia. He was from Chicago, I said, how'd he end up there? When the market crashed he was on tour, he told me, was cleaned out when the banks went under. His band was working its way through the South. When he couldn't pay them, they jumped ship. Didn't even have enough money to blow his horn. So he stayed in the town where he'd gone broke, took work as a cook and janitor. Hospitals, I think. He cleaned bedpans, I'm sure. Man, it's inspiring, the insults to real talent this world can cook up.

For the day or so I stayed on in town, he referred to himself as the King. That was just exactly Steve's sense of humor. King O, he'd say, pointing at himself, no crown.

This was during my last trip home. Even though my family lived in the cemetery outside Maryhurst, I still made a point to duck in once a year to check in on him.

When his sister Deena called the following January to tell me what happened, I hardly needed an explanation. Someone had knocked on the door of that second floor apartment out back of that last house he was living in; they had tried the doorknob; light opened on a kitchen scene with no furnishings to speak of—one fork, spoon, bowl and plate stacked neatly in the sink. In the bedroom he lay on his side, in a condition too easy to imagine, close as he was to a posthumous color when I last saw him. Such a skinny, harsh, vulnerable wit. Inconsolable for reasons he couldn't fathom. It was just the fact of his existence, he supposed, to be down on his luck and on himself. Surely the coroner called Deena and had her stand there, trembling, to confirm the identity of the body he pulled out of the cold. King Doe, I can almost hear Steve say, poking a finger to his chest. Surely he'd be even funnier now in person, now that he was gone.

Is it wrong to admit I love the man more now that he's gone? No more bad habits, disagreeable opinions to get in the way. Just the pure, general idea of him? Good, humble, defeated beyond measure. The service was small and might as well have been held in a parking lot. A priest intoned sweet nothings over the body, some people from the funeral home closed the casket, carried it onto rollers which sucked it into the back of the hearse. The motorcade only drove three blocks. A motorcade of two. From there the old mission's cemetery took over: several acres of headstones expanding from some unidentifiable center, breaking yards of new ground each year. The first person had been put to earth two hundred years ago, and now Steve was joining up with that illustrious company, a small bit of decoration on the land. A neat stone with his name and dates, three bunches of flowers arranged around it. Only three of us present—Deena, myself, and an older woman, a secretary from St. Aloysius' who shared cigarettes with him on their lunch break.

We had to hide out back behind the generator, the woman told us, couldn't be a bad example for the kids. Deena and I had asked her to lunch afterwards. She didn't have much to say about Steve other than he didn't always look so well, but was always, always kind, never not ready with a wisecrack. He was good company, she said, and, thank god, never pretended he wasn't anywhere he wasn't. I felt a heavy pull of recognition when she said that. What kind of a friend was I? How many times had I waited for word from him instead of just driving down for a weekend or sparing an hour to call? There's not much that can account for a person who knows there are few people in the world available to think about him. And that in all likelihood they're busy with their lives, and grateful for the distraction, hardly justifies any sore feelings towards them. It takes effort to attain some measure of relevance in the estimation of most people, and it has been the end of many a strong man and woman to try and sustain that kind of attention. Exhaustion is the natural end for anyone with no luck but more than their share of ambition. Steve was stoic on the matter. He kept to himself, earned his keep, walked a short while on the path of least resistance. He didn't leave a will. Deena donated his belongings to St. Vincent DePaul. The mattress we burned. Or better put: handed over to the city to burn. Horrible to think, but I thought it, why couldn't we have just cremated him, bed and all?

After lunch, the secretary left us with this one last story. Laughed just as she caught herself remembering it.

Man did have a wicked sense to him, she said. Once late in the spring before school was out for summer, he and I had walked out back for a smoke break. This was about the time these Japanese beetles were all around, eating up people's rosebushes, mucking up windshields. Well Steve was smoking and talking about what I can't remember, when one of them beetles lands right on his cigarette, right there while it's hanging from his lips. "Hold on there," I told him and made to brush it off, but he put me off. Just stood there still as he could manage, like he was waiting to see how long he could keep it there or what it'd do next. And you know what? It clung there a good five minutes. Him standing there perfectly still with his hands raised on either side of his head, like he was listening to someone calling him from far off. Like he was balanced on something and trying hard not to fall off. These things—I don't know if you've ever seen one—they're big. Thick, fat, black, meaty bugs. Big razor wings, shaped kind of like sundials. Anybody with any sense would've flicked the thing right off and jumped a good foot back. But nope, he just stood there. Almost like he was showing it who wasn't afraid of it. The thing didn't budge either. They generally come and go as they please. But this one didn't move a bit 'til he raised a finger, real slow, gave me a wink. Took a long slow drag then blew a bunch of smoke its way. That thing, it dropped right off to the ground. Now this is what made Mr. Steve different from most folks. What'd he do but crouch down, apologize in the most polite voice, lay that cigarette right next to it until it climbed back on? He stood back up as he was before, that bug on his cigarette, smiling with all of that right between his lips. It doesn't sound like much but at the time it was one of the queerest, sweetest things I'd ever seen come off a man.

Deena smiled at us and raised a hand, said, I'd seen him do that one too. When we were kids. Not with a beetle but with a pill worm. It crawled right off his cigarette and up his nose and set him off on a sneezing fit.

That caught a laugh from all of us. We were standing in the parking lot. Our shadows were crisp and long, and pointed off into the direction of our cars.

I hadn't seen him do anything comparable, I told them, but then remembered. No wait, I had, in a way. Once, when we were younger, on a drunk I'd fallen on the steps to my apartment; he came running back down the stairs to get me. Instead of helping me off my knees, he'd hefted me up over his shoulder, carried me the rest of the way. Almost clipped my head against the doorframe. When he set me down on the couch I remembered telling him how amazed I was someone so skinny could carry a body heavy as me. No worries, he said, it's no problem at all carrying someone heavier than you. It's just a matter of picking them up. Get them on your shoulder and the rest is smooth walking. I had my doubts then. It didn't sound plausible. But what right did I have to say his theory was untested, when my laying there was proof to the contrary?

Deena and the old lady laughed at that, both pulling cigarettes from a pack I'd produced from my pocket. One for the bugs, I said, catching each of us off the flame of the lighter.

I can still remember the look he gave me, not bemused exactly, not irritated. The strangely serene look of someone who'd ran a mile just so he could turn around and look at it.

When I thanked him again, he smiled, shook his head the usual way, said *the first time is a favor, the second a service.* And then, with a dry forgiving laugh: *No worries.*

It was dusk. The restaurant sign mimicked the sunset, cherry red. Deena took her heels off, held them. We stood there a bit and talked some more, but none of it was as important or worth mentioning. Afterwards driving back to the motel and the interstate and the thirteen hours home, I looked in the rear view and saw the usual cars and promised myself almost without saying it: never again.

PART 2

THREAD AND SWORD

"Živjeli!" In English, you can raise your glasses to it: Cheers! In Bosnian, the exact translation is an imperative, a bracing injunction: Live! After they said cheers they said live, in a language only two of them understood.

Gordon leaned across the table to Mr. Bursač. "Do they raise their glasses in Bosnia as well?"

Mr. Bursač, bashful, pale but cheerful—all three adjectives he would use to describe any math professor like himself—narrowed his eyes and matched them with a mock-skeptical smile. This was supposed to look like thinking.

"In the country, yes. In Mostar, yes. But not in Sarajevo. Everywhere else we'll do this," he said, levitating the pint above his head. "But in the city even before the whole Serbian mess, they did differently. Not everyone's a Christian, but when they raise glasses they stop three times before Živjeli. First, they press here, at the heart; then next, the forehead. Then they hold it over the crown of their heads. And when they yell *toast!* whoever doesn't spill a drop gets to drink first. But everyone's head gets wet."

Gordon held his glass up and made a quip about his rim halo and smiled and said, "Just like Damocles."

Mr. Bursač nodded in surprised agreement, his whole body rocking. "Yes! Except we swallow the sword!" The bar was loud with people, Afrobeat on the jukebox, so when he smiled he had to yell through the smile.

"One thing, though. I should mention. After the war, they changed the toast. Same as before, with their glass they would touch their chest, their forehead, and then hold it up. But now they would say "Živ" at the heart, "jel" at the head, and "li" last. Easier not to spill your beer, no? Fewer syllables."

"That's true," Gordon said. "But the fewer the syllables, the louder you can yell." And just then an exposed mix of suspicion and embarrassment came over him.

WHO'S THE BETTER MAN?

Some rivers will never run through it. The eye of a needle, the country where your fathers cease to be born... These days, rivers are becoming rarer and rarer. Most of the ones I've seen from the speeding length of an interstate look like the snail-trails of cities. Cincinnati, New York, Paris... The snails didn't die or disappear inside their shell but multiplied by the thousands into millions. Whole generations of disappearing and self-replenishing snails. But the trails they leave behind, their city crawling in pace, never moving forward or backward or detailing the intricacy of a leaf, always glisten as if they were traced hugely on the ground just yesterday. Ageless.

My father had this silly saying about rivers, that was really more about his ability to conquer the rabbit traps of time through kissing: better to swim in a river than to believe in it. Better to swim in something that has a sense of direction but no purpose, than sail a perfect yacht across it. My father always had more luck than power—was a bricklayer for more than half his life—but when it came to completing his half of a kiss, was able beyond misfortune. He liked fishing as well, though was never particularly skilled at it. After the fourth beer he'd inevitably lay his reel aside and lean over the boat's edge to scoop the water with his hands. May not have caught many fish that way, but did snatch the vanishing wobble of his reflection many times.

His favorite game was to sit there leaning over himself, and like a gunslinger see if he could draw and drink his beer faster than nature. Nature was always half a half second too slow. But me? By the time the bottle's touched my lips my reflection's already on its second beer. Now you tell me, even though I'm young and handsome, and he's too broken to be happy, who's the better man?

THESE ARTISTS

"These artists are crazy, selfish creatures. I swear, they'll take a swing at anything that denies their existence. I believe in love. I don't need anybody to talk me into it. I don't need fatal, excruciatingly sensitive prisms surgically implanted in my brain. What the world needs, or, let's downgrade the ambition of that statement, what Chicago needs, or better yet, what the Northwest Side needs, is more sweetness and fellowship and less drive to drag all that through the aesthetic eye of the needle.

"I'm on a very high soapbox, I know. But it has wings. It's a flying soapbox and is the next best thing to a magic carpet, which must exist just as much nowadays as they did in pre-modern Persia. But the thing to remember is, that box once housed many neatly stacked bars of soap. And they're gone now. They cleaned the soiled, slick bodies of people standing alone or two to a shower. Now those people are as alive as they are anonymous. They're ancient to the speculating mind—obscure. But seeing as I'm no artist, no great thinker, or even a serviceable salesman, I have to enter the loving wavelength sideways; with my fingertips, I touch my face. There are more people in there than I can ever wonder. Sinners and skinflints and salt-spitting gossips. Brief smilers, thoughtful losers. Geniuses of disposition vanishing perfectly into their tact.

"What I don't feel rising to the surface are the famous names. But that doesn't mean they're not in there too. Rather they're back in their prime element. Among the rabble they drew bright energy from, and to whom they were, according to their wishes, most rightfully returned."

THE SAFE ONES

I'm the kind of person who has to prove to himself that he has a will. Usually this involves not sleeping with very beautiful married women who text me at three o'clock in the morning. The last quivering grain of courtliness in the Western Hemisphere appears then, like the fabled angel on the head of a pin. It's a communal resource—like the tooth fairy or God—and makes brief appearances to men and women in crises of temptation. I'm picturing it now, eyes closed, our little conscience creature teleporting all night from the heads of penises to the shawls of clitorises, cajoling the potent haunches of lust back into neat, quaint curls.

It's enough to make a man reach into his boxers while brushing his teeth, to flop out the innocent criminal wick from its lair.

Moronically hard, it points up, like a gun, to my head.

The whole animal kingdom rigid and blooded! Ridiculous! For this men of power and unfinished empires have squandered poise and brought diseases, bad luck, and loveless pregnancies into the world.

Somewhere there's probably a woman doing much the same, barefooted smacking through her kitchen or bathroom in her underwear. Then that mischievous giddiness in the genitals releases its ecstatic poison up her spine. Suddenly, like a waking zombie, her free hand is traveling at the speed of bedsheets to munch every last sliver of her so-called erotic brains.

Masturbation is a saintly discipline, I've long thought.

Between answering the text message and saying yes to the cheating orgasm and rubbing out its potentially destructive version of the world forever, there appears a little imp—psychopomp of the last incorruptible wink of human goodness. The man stands there, prick in one hand, cell phone in the other. The woman stands as well, weighing the pleasures of a buzzing cell against those of her lover calling. It's then the Safe One appears, glowing, calm, climbing atop the most receptive parts of their genitals.

"Think of his wife. Think of her husband," it says. "Remember the children you aren't imagining. They're all here, if you can believe it, waiting to be launched into this room by your orgasm."

It's then you know your moral duty is to give flesh to its own. And you'll do so. But not before closing your eyes and humping them without compromise, with imaginary joy.

SEVEN MILES OVER PRUSSIA

Prussia, we learned, was composed of three quietly interlocking countries: Estonia, Latvia, and Lithuania. The typography of which was imaginary. Never having Googled a photograph or spoken with a living Latvian, we could only imagine the land itself was a shared continuum of mountains, rivers, and innocently ornate meadows. But did snowdrops grow there, we wondered.

We had been studying the parts of flowers, and since flowers were unfaithful citizens, we guessed anything small and white that bloomed in the winter could do as well in Europe as in America. An inch of snow had fallen two nights ago. One day of slightly heated sunlight had melted the surface enough for the evening cold to harden it. But the muscles of flower stalks are stronger than frozen water: snowdrops that had been working from the ground all week continued their burrowing to sunlight.

Vernation, the arrangement of emerging leaves relative to each other; the outer flutters of a flower, the perianth—technical terms for the shyness of human involvement. On our afternoon walk, the neighborhood still under a trance of barely falling snow, we spoke a bit about our plans for the year, about our frustrations and troubles, and the vernation of listening into confession held us in mutual thrall. Casually so: we were only talking. We externalized ourselves into each other's trust. Our nodding and small responses were fragile but sturdy, not unlike the layered twists of flowers. We floated through an understanding we left behind as we walked.

We'll never visit any of these countries, you said. The "P" preceding "Russia" is definitely its perianth. I was sucked body and soul all the way through sudden laughter. You were always like that, supporting and dissecting reality with a pun or two. As for me, I could only pursue the topic at hand with a little scrub of science: "snowdrops may or may not grow there, but I can tell you one thing about them. Galantamine is an active agent in them, as well as in daffodils. They use it to treat Alzheimer's patients. It slows the degeneration of the brain, but doesn't stop it, I think."

That last part, that qualification, "I think," wherever it appears, makes all the difference. You smiled. You were on to something. And of course the comment I was waiting for arrived fully informed. "The wonderful thing, if you think about it, is that someone would name all these tough beauties after Narcissus."

OLD GIRL

I met a woman once who was convinced and tried to rope me into believing she was the reincarnation, or rather the reconfiguration of Lao Tzu. In reality the first coming of Lao Tzu on earth, since it is widely believed among a very tiny select group of specialists that the sage never truly existed as a personage in the first place, but more likely was a fiction devised for the convenience of creating a text, an anthology of advice and covert criticism of Confucian philosophy and policy, assembled by a group of anti-legalist scholars seeking patronage. This was how the Christian god was invented, after all, so why not?

But none of us had considered the likeliness that a literary construction several millennia old could come to sudden, albeit obscure fruition as a brunette of moderate height, with an easy, raspy voice and a smile that could turn pebbles into pennies. That is: which was capable of minor feats of alchemy, ones that led to no advantage. She spoke in small, tightly constructed phrases which created the effect of wisdom, several concussive insights or observations which rippled from their centers and left a satisfied expansive silence in their wake. Whether she believed she was an Old Boy, a venerable Chinese sage, or a woman in her mid-twenties who had mastered the tricky art of suggestiveness, who knows.

She bore herself with the ease of someone who already knew the full design of her life, of where it would lead and what it would compel her to abandon along the way, so she might keep moving. And that quality of gentle fatalism lent her an authority which was all the more delightfully unusual when it was compelled to lay back its head and laugh. Which she did frequently. Never at jokes or quick witticisms, more at the atmosphere of absurdity produced by certain situations. Of a policeman made to stoop and pick up a hotdog that slipped from its bun to the sidewalk. Of a woman covering her mouth as she talked, to shield herself from her own bad breath. It didn't matter, it seemed, whether she was crazy or deluded or guilty of constructing a joke only she could remain inside of—the joke was at no one's expense, and the delusion bore no purpose but to calm and fascinate. The effect was the same, no matter the motivation. Here was a woman whom none of us knew very well due to the strategic silence she created between herself and others, and the effect was contradictory: while it conveyed an aura of importance, it just as quickly dispersed it. She illustrated the wisdom often made available by accepting the prospect that no one, no matter the effort, would ever know her. It rendered her a benevolent figure in everyone's memory, especially my own.

That we could look back fondly, without honestly loving her, as if she were a grandmother who had reached old age before we had entered the kaleidoscopic awkwardness of adolescence, when everything is memorable because it is painful. The fact that she hurt no one and kept her own counsel: maybe this was the thing.

LUCIDA

The professions of lost mystics on the matter are inconclusive: does beauty lead the way to something relevant? Which is understandable; they only specialize in a certain, rarefied kind of beauty—that which does not die. So by implication does this mean what is fated to die is ugly? There's no direct word from them on the matter, though every now and then one will say 'flesh is evil.' Even to the first honest ear that caught word of such a sentiment, it must have sounded contradictory. "All that must die is evil." Inarguable, yes, that it's an unfortunate condition—that what is granted the marvel of growth and change, of heft and tactility—must, by that manner, exist past ripeness and decay. To arrive at these thoughts, flesh was necessary: it sponsored the very earliest thought of some unimpeachable creator, whether organized as a divine personality with opinions and preferences, or dispersed among many lesser agents, each answerable to a specific mystery (where does rain come from? how does the sun not devour the sky?). God was the reason for death; but beforehand, death was the provocation that led to God. Each arrives at their own reason, and even among those reasons, countless inflections with which to express it; but death, it remained the same.

Everything, being ugly, discouraged vanity. Mirrors with true depth would not reflect the flesh but examine it. The finest aspiration in this evil and this flesh would be to express it as if it were a way which led to the impossible, its own perfection, something symmetrical and designed to discard life in those very places where it turned on itself choking on its own excess energies. The bodies, the faces of everyone who is not deathless: there is where beauty can be studied and sought after and entered, if only before the blink of an eye. Grooming one's hair, one's eyelashes, skin, tautening the muscles of one's arms and stomach…to shape the inherent ugliness of flesh so it might transcend itself and master the very terms of its existence. Just as all beauty descended from that first revulsion, all flesh would be fashioned to contend with it. Of course, there are very few surviving photographs of those who spoke with such ecstatic engagement—with the Light, Disembodied Mind, the Template. Perhaps those were only words, or excited claims from madness, or poetry misapplied as transcendental vision. They praised beauty before the invention of the camera. So how, then, could they perish from handling it?

SNOWS FROM THE DEEP

The loneliest man in Philadelphia, I've always thought, must be
William Penn. Dead a few hundred years and still he stands tall, a
bronze statue atop the highest turret of City Hall. How many generations of pigeons have spent their bowels off the brim of his hat,
to streak down his waistcoat and legs of his breeches? It's a cliché
to mention it to anyone within the city's limits, but for nearly two
centuries there was a gentleman's agreement that no building in
the city's center would be allowed to grow higher than the top of
his hat. Vertical real estate is cheaper than the horizontal kind—so
surely that promise was bound to be broken. In the late 80's the city
founder's view of his people was blotted out by an office building
at One Liberty Place. Now, instead of floating high above them, a
representative human being, he was merely sculpted metal, and not
even the most expensive kind, a "state shoe" statue. Grubbing cigarettes, frozen at crosswalks, sluffing fruits and vegetables in quiet
bags from the nearby market...in the flesh, the diverse yield of the
past he helped establish and encourage flourishes in every direction

as actual people.

Three blocks away there is a bake sale, nine kinds of cookies arranged on trays, three men selling them, each awarding any sweet-tooth who stops by with a red ribbon tiny enough to tie around one's pinky finger—though these are made to be fastened to a lapel. Brotherly love in a kingdom of used snow...two months and The Man On High will be covered with it. Everything mountainous and white as far as the eye can see, though—being an idea and not a man—he knows the promise of an avalanche, while always there, is not enough to jar a sleeping monster from the slopes. With the knowledge: Spring always comes before the warmth.

MEN OF SHIVELY

A small, busted one-floor house at the end of a stubby street near the water treatment plant beyond the south of town. Mr. Washington and I knock on the door. It's three weeks till Christmas. The wreath hanging there, at eye level, like a holly bush chewed up and spat out, splat, right there on the door. A lady answers. "Come in, honey, I'm too old to smile."

We've come to tape plastic to the windows, chalk the edges, affix rubber floor runners to the doors, what they call "winterizing" a house. Funny, evocative, isn't it? The irony isn't lost on the house: it's colder in there than it is outside, because heat knows a thing or two about rising, but cold knows even more about finding a way in and staying put. The living room is lined with old couches, a big-screen T.V. (never a busted old house we winterized that *didn't* have a large television in it), wet tinsel stringy on thick dirty carpet. She smokes through her dark, puffy, almost punished eyelids, and asks if we fix leaky ceilings as well. Points up with her cigarette and there it is. An almost casual magic trick: hadn't noticed it there before, and who *doesn't* catch sight of a brown watery bruise like that, spreading just left of center on the ceiling, a Rorschach ring of stale Coca Cola. "Nope," says Mr. Washington. Takes off his ball cap to talk to her. "Well, I appreciate you looking up," she says, smiling. Football highlights are replaying on Sports Center. An oxygen tank rests under a stuffed animal beside her. Had she hidden it? The one thing she doesn't need us looking at, smoking to the detriment of her lungs in a house that lets in all manner of breezes.

We set to work. She talks. She tells us about how bad she has been, her words, and has really put her poor shell, again, her words, through all kinds of hell. "I won't even tell you the kind of things I smoked and snorted." Mr. Washington tells her, "Well, at least now you won't have to worry about no drafty house." Her grandchildren are at school. Her daughter is at work. Toys are piled in two distinct corners: one for boys, one for girls. The bedrooms are overrun with excesses of living. Four heavy comforters mound off beds and bank against the walls to climb them. Mr. Washington measures and cuts plastic, I measure and tape sills. Three hours later, done. Any smoke blown into a room will stay there. Amassing a private cloud. Three hours closer to Christmas.

Between crimpled blinds hairy with dust, "ready for a shave," jokes Mr. Washington, the grass between houses wasted flat on their yards, mealy as papier-mâché dissolving in rain. "All done," says Mr. Washington, shouldering a roll of plastic, his tool box in the other hand. "I left a little tape here for you, in case some comes loose. Should be enough to mend any leaks you might have." "Don't think I can't call you two again," she winks, "if that happens?" "No, mam, we're busy men," Mr. Washington tells her. "Can't see that happening.

You live too far out. Would take us another year to make our way out here." She laughs. "Well you're saying something there." Then, pushing the stuffed animal off and patting the tank next to her, wedding ring catching the steel and pinging, a word for no age that we're living: "If this house has another year, we'll see you. Now get."

OLD HALLOWS

So many sunsets behind her. So many ugly, anonymous mountains. So many people met in the loose middle ground between days then rarely seen again, and if seen, bearing their features to show how they've changed. She was carefree once; and that no direction in life seemed so important that she had to choose it was a cause for drunken layabout celebration. With minimal pain of labor to pay for pleasures, she followed the slog of friends from night to night, and each one with a plan they all fully intended to deviate from, and together in small groups, or one on one, discussed the hand-me-downs called Hopes and Loves, then earmarked them for later reference as Dreams.

Music was of core importance. Up from the ground itself it had come, each band wriggling to the surface like worms after rain. The melodies were for emotions, the lyrics for understanding. Even if they were so plain and crude they weren't the proper vessels for conveying meaning: all the better to sing along with a melody and learn that most shortcomings can be forgiven if they're written on the breath of a human voice. But what about an inhuman one? What would that sound like, where would it come from? The words of their favorite songs, the ones they sang along to with windows rolled down on a fall day, college providing a crumbling routine around them, the trees flush with the winds of a future winter, a voice that does not have a mother or father tied to it, or a chronology, or body that it can be ashamed or proud of, that can be mistreated or engorged with animal riches, a voice that is older than the years it extracts from them, as they listen.

She appeared at parties on its arm. She disappeared on holiday breaks to follow it back to her family, who lived in a town some three hours away. There were two boys she kept in her head for a month, both held there by an ache not even high school had taught her to be excited about. A crush—was that it? Two of them? She rarely felt unified as one person, which she thought was what you had to become before someone older than you considers you, without a thought otherwise, to be a woman. Just two girls splitting off in two directions, each with a single wardrobe to draw from.

So much was full of small, comfortable terror back then. To say the right thing or the wrong, to be the appropriate person in the appropriate moment. To not even know why this rendered her young. So much free time to fight against and from it fashion some kind of brighter identity, a thesis which encapsulated the arguments behind all this fun. Important to have it, to be it. To spread it around like summer. To enjoy and not understand, because contemplation is a product of scarcity, which age will bring to a calming, claustrophobic then calming relaxed conclusion in you. A lifetime of jobs waited for each of them in the silent future. Like dozens of straws descending from the sky, each sucking up one of them and then retracting into the heavens, where they seek advancement and set up retirement accounts and combine with spouses to divide later as children, at last in accord with the natural order of things.

When she thought back ten, twenty years, she was often met with some brief flits of visual memory, recombined and distorted. A weekend trip to a cabin. Drinking in a dorm room. Walking arm and arm with a friend beneath tall trees imploding with a strong fall wind. Those long stretches of afternoons spent doing nothing, imagining how certain scenarios would play out if she were suddenly to meet a bit of gossip on the street, and act on it. Eating chili from a Styrofoam bowl in a small campus cafeteria. Throwing away clothes that no longer "felt" like her. A sobering daydream emotion—to be lonely for oneself, as one once was in the past, unformed and messy, when there was so much she could be and so little to keep her from becoming it, if only she'd choose, with sudden firmness, yes, that's what I want, to go that way, and do these things, and admit these particular limitations into the fluid element of what I plan to keep thriving on. Not a foolish ache, or a lost one. To fantasize about the past, not how it could have been, but how it was. That there could be more of it, unused pockets of it, buried in the folds of its fickle engine, the brain; though it's not her brain she's loving, but the whole world absorbed by it, imprinted there in miniature facsimiles of lightness and boredom.

Funny how the smell of trees in October could convince not this brain but her body, that maybe there is more of herself to remember. Or maybe not. Though the longer she makes time this way, the less it seems to matter. A good day is and was a good day.

Regardless of which direction you take it. What it takes back, you didn't give it. And then did.

THE SECOND SISTER

She'd wanted to console me in the earliest minutes of my coming to the knowledge that she did not love me, had maybe never loved me, much less delineated to herself exactly what bundle of intuitions might constitute love, though this time, she said, she was certain, she did not love me anymore. To add that one last condition—*anymore*—didn't sweeten the bite she had just taken out of me. She was the one with the mouthful, anyways, so she might as well get it over with and begin chewing me, either way I'm not going to taste even the smallest hint of its sweetness, if there is any.

I had to sit there, like a cliché on a bench, in the park, and of course a park in the middle of town, people walking their dogs and their children around us. It occurred to me almost immediately, in the aftermath of being bitten, I'll be damned, she knew what she was doing, had chosen this spot explicitly as the place to tell me. Is it more or less humiliating to be held in check in moments of weakness surrounded by a constant flow of strangers? Maybe it's only a flourish of lyricism. *Here I am, suddenly, someone you don't know, though you thought you did, and don't I now seem to resemble all these other people passing by, smoking cigarettes and talking through their collars, led along by their cell phones? I could stand up, step away, and would you even be able to tell me apart from them?* What could be crueler than a well-placed expression of wistfulness or wisdom, when you're sitting there, freshly dumped, smoldering in your own foolishness?

Anyway, she was decent at least, she spared me the platitudes, but since it was expected that she try to make some effort to console me, which let's be honest is only an obligatory gesture made by someone who fancies themselves a decent person, not just a strong, self-possessed, handsome woman, but a person with a tactful sense of balance, which says: take any one thing away, you must replace it with something of equal weight and significance. So she folded her hands in her lap and waited for me to calm down and then, when it was clear any appeal or plea on my part would be fruitless, told me a story.

A story of two sisters, twins, who, having reached middle age with almost identical lives, realize they are bored and to amend the problem decide to switch identities. One has two young children and a husband, another a long-term boyfriend and two children from a previous marriage. One thinks life would be more fulfilling as an undivorced mother of two, the other looks back with nostalgia on her days as an unwed woman, free to come and go through one man's life or another's. Their ruse works. Each dresses the part. Behaves according to the roles they assume. Change their hairstyles. One afternoon, meeting in a park, they trade cars and drive home. A week later both women report their partners show a sudden peak in attraction, though they've hardly made an effort to lure them from their clothes. The children, strangely enough, hardly seem to notice; a mother is a mother, apparently, and for the first month after the switch they ignore, that is, accept, their surrogate mom without reservations, as long as the food is cooked, the table set, and the forks and knives cleaned afterwards.

After a few months, the divorced sister mentions she might like to trade back, but the married one, newly free, having recently broken up with the boyfriend she acquired, enjoyed the time alone, the weekends when she sent her children to their father's, when she could play a fully divorced woman calmly alone and self-reliant in her apartment, sleeping late and taking walks, listening to the rain on the windowpanes. In short, she said no. No, I don't want to go back, and what could her sister do? She was bound by mutual silence and the threat of guilt, of full exposure, to keep in line with the life she had acquired and make the best of it and see it to its natural end. To break the news to either family that they had been depending on a false mother would surely ruin everyone, and most of all turn their children against them. So they kept on their allotted trajectories for thirty, forty years. The children grew up into adults, that is, strangers, and stood up, stepped away, and became indistinguishable from the rush of the crowd. Their partners melted away like weight acquired during pregnancy, and vanished into either disease or senility or divorce. Eventually their lives were almost identical, and the irony they derived from observing them was enough to cause them to nod and laugh. Alone, retired, living in modestly sized homes, why not switch back? What they gain or lose, it might be amusing to find out. So, trading houses and pensions, they resumed the pattern of habits they had so long ago abandoned. But still, the question: who would die first? Who would, in the end, be happier? Left with only each other to trade lives with, would it be better if they could resemble someone else entirely?

MOVING WATER

He had no way of knowing what it meant to be kind, at least this is what our mother had said, not as an excuse, but as the beginning of some explanation. Our mother had married not a cruel man, but an unimaginative one; one of those many half-souls who wander the earth looking like people, but bearing themselves with much less conscious weight. He did not beat her. He did not raise a harsh word against her, at least not willingly. He simply overlooked the subtle presences of a person, when they share a room with you, occupy a bed with you, leave the house at seven and return to it sometimes at six, sometimes at eight. This was back in the years before the memories of now younger women were activated, borne from all time and their mothers' wombs into the many attitudes of baby, the sleepless baby, the crying baby, the compulsively hungry: back when a woman alone in a house with no man but two children was a shameful thing, a popular neighborhood example of failure.

Our father had left for an auto job in Detroit. Two envelopes of money later, no letter, just a handwritten note, "Be back soon." He disappeared entirely from human record. It wasn't strictly true that he had left us. He had merely set out with the best of intentions, to find a job, provide for the family long-distance, but had somewhere along the way trailed off. The three letters he sent in six months' time, those dotted the way out into the unremitting enormity of the cosmos like a set of very small, private ellipses. The third letter was long, containing no money, our mother had never let us touch it or see it, much less read it, though once on my tenth birthday and on our insistence she had recited a passage from it. "The trees here are a little smaller," she read, impersonating her late, still living husband, our father, "but that's just about the only difference." How many women in those years let go of their husbands and months later opened similar letters? And how many, then, did as our mother did and took work in a factory, out of necessity but also out of some kind of primal nostalgia? Into factories their husbands went, into them they too shall go, to find them, or men similar in mind and habit.

Our mother met our father's lookalike within a year, a tall, busted, brawny man who had long managed to fashion his aggression into a form of confidence. He did not strike her then, in that first year, just as much as he didn't strike her later, but silences are just as solid as fists and, as the saying goes, often strike deeper. She married a big chunk of silence, and who knows, maybe because she believed it would be easier. A man who's quiet doesn't lie, he doesn't need to. He leaves nothing to subvert or erase. He says nothing, offers nothing more than his being near at any given moment, and though this might not be taken as a commitment, it could be accepted as a kind of promise.

His indifference was consistent, and his salary was honest. Our mother married him in June three months after meeting him, their wedding day uneventful and sunny. He moved into the house and the bedroom, and acknowledged the presence of a stepson and daughter. He was large and sat at the table like a teacher, but one with no lesson to go over, though for a while we watched for one, as if his dull largeness was the preamble to some moral he would eventually impart to us. But blankness was his only hidden muscle. He flexed it behind our eyes and in our heads, while distracting us with the ugly hugeness of his biceps hanging like slabs at the table. To see such big hands wield such tiny utensils, it was not funny, it was an admonishment, a chiding of the helplessness of small things, us included. Our mother fed him and occasionally he smiled and sometimes we would be surprised by how short our mother could be with him. Why criticize him when he had said nothing wrong, having said nothing?

She was not so silent or small herself. It was the germ of revenge in her blood which our father had left in her, having left her, a contagion straight from a city to the north, which she called Detroit. She made this man, large as he was, something she could not forgive, though he had done little to offend her. Only later, when we had ceased being stepsons and had grown old enough to look back into the past as a kind of frightening machine of consciousness, did we see how our mother had understood more of her life than it had been willing to give her: that an unwillingness to offend was not a virtue, but often a symptom of disinterest, and as a man and woman build mutual habits on such shifty ground, the foundations are bound to give way. Within two winters she was, and we were, alone again. And this man, his factory full of quiet, he was given back to the universe like some contaminated fish. After that, our mother did not use makeup as much, and her naturally curly hair remained so, and the dresses she wore were progressively more practical and identical, replicating each day the same bare effect of simplicity and cleanliness and carefulness. Who would say this was the final fashion choice of a kind woman? Or would it matter, as long as she was a thoughtful mother? Often the two are not mutually inclusive. Just as second husbands are often not reliable improvements. When winter ends, the ground knows to show it. Green all the way from Mississippi to Washington. And miles of moving water between.

PART 3

AUSTRALIA '71

This photograph is all man now. That's the first thought that occurs when I look at him, my father, thin as paper, forty years ago and still balding at the camera. Flip it over. On the back, a written inscription—*Australia, '71*. Flip it back and there's Australia. Scrub brush, sun-kill sky, a baked horizon speckled with stunted trees. My father's dressed in his fatigues even though he's on leave, rifle in one hand, his weight shifted mostly to one side to offset what he's hoisting up with his other arm: a sizable kangaroo, fingers hooked into its snout, its whole weight hanging on its nostrils.

I know some of the backstory on the trip. Which brings along its own strange effects—to know the details of a trip he took before he met my mother, a good five years before I was born. It was his first leave; his company had been given two options—Japan or Australia. For someone who between the ages of ten and eighteen had watched as many Westerns as he had, it was a no-brainer. They were given a list of names, people who had signed up to welcome Americans into their homes, my father found a man who owned a farm just south of Goyder's Line; the description promised hunt-ing—wild boar, kangaroo. Why someone who ran convoys through the mountains to Quan Tri would want, in his spare time, time off from being shot at so he could hunt, heave hay bales off a wagon, is beyond me. Nostalgia could be the reason. He'd grown up on a farm. He'd hunted rabbits and coyote. He was accustomed to in-vesting himself in very specific tasks that promised a definitive end point. He would be out in the sun, in a dry climate, at night no mortar rounds would fall out of the sky and threaten to take off his head. What could be more relaxing? Then I find this photograph and hold it up, the irony achieves perfect symmetry. A corpse in hand for each of us. The kangaroo, I notice, is wounded above the heart, a smear of blood across its breast.

His brothers and sisters attest: he was once fairly sensitive. Always very serious. The smallest of the brothers but the oldest. So when they began to grow up and work alongside him on the farm he had to push twice as hard to match them. More than once he worked until he collapsed. His brothers Paul and Chance were ei-ther wiser or lazier, but didn't go that path. They did the work that was expected of them, graduated high school and went to college, smoked pot and chased girls. To fulfill the role of the Serious One, my father was willing to go to extremes previously unthought of by almost anyone—he would *join* the Army, he would become an officer, he would head over to Vietnam as quickly as he could. Not to sift the bush for Vietcong, he wasn't that foolish. No, he'd insert himself into the situation sideways, become a man of the supply line, running twenty truck convoys from jungle to jungle. It took his first experience of seeing a man blown up, needlessly, uselessly—a box of grenades dropped while unloading a truck—before his gut could be fully educated on the matter of what exists between zones of life and death. A very taut, violently shining ligament: Ceaseless Pain. That day, there at his feet, screaming in the dirt, he saw it and thought, Not for me.

The first opportunity he had to leave country, he did.

Photographs from that time show a young man, half my age, with a look of desperate jovial aggression. In each he wears a mustache, thick, brown, styled, I'd like to imagine, after Charles Bronson. These photographs are a man now; but aside from the natural effects of aging, he bears only one notable difference: his staunch refusal to hide any part of his face. Beards and goatees and mustaches are for cowards; they camouflage the fear running close to the surface of the human face so elegantly you'd be convinced the face itself is beyond self-doubt, half-animal in its instinctual commitment to combat and disfigurement and misery. These photos date from what we like to call his "Lost Mustache Period." In half he appears a little drunk, though I know that's not the case. You'd be hard pressed to find a man born south of the Mason-Dixon who was charmed less by the promise of a drink. Only after looking at him, photo after photo, posed in his barracks or outside a mess hall, does it occur to me, maybe it's just that, what was driven from his face by the presence of defensive hair, fear forced to collect and concentrate in his eyes, so everything he looked at was dominated by it.

This one, for example. No date on the back. He sits on a wall of sandbags, in a bunker. Several men on either side of him, drinking. Shirt sleeves rolled up taut mid-bicep. His gun out of its holster, raised to his head, pressed to his temple, a campy crazed smile distracting the camera from the plain pained look of his eyes. The kind of eyes that say: *I'm a mistake.*

Maybe he looked at those Polaroids the next morning and thought, *Is it that plain to see?* And then, something more natural and conventional: *I need a vacation.* That whole first tour he kept a very controlled regimen of communication with friends and family. Letters were preferable, if he had the time. Something about the act of narrowing his sense of the world to a piece of paper and a half hour of quiet, it relaxed the nerves so something more tender could open a little beneath them. Of course, he would never describe it that way. It would take someone thoroughly removed from his situation to think of him as given over to such thoughts, of prizing such things, the prospects of turning over something soft inside of him. On the contrary, I hear the letters are quite boring. The ones his family didn't misplace or eventually throw away can't attest to this, but the ones that were found years later, according to my sister, were so uneventful they were almost not worth keeping. He may not have written many anyway. By his third month in country he began recording letters on cassette; but given his reputation as a talker, I can only imagine these were similar to his letters. My grandmother couldn't stand to listen to them. She didn't trust their mundanity—there were men with guns, Communists, aimed in the direction of that voice coming from the tape player, her eldest son's voice, and no amount of talk about baseball or barracks humor could convince her otherwise. Some of them she didn't even finish listening to. She just handed them over to the younger kids so they could record songs from the radio.

Given the spotty prospects of finding a cassette or a letter, it'd be best to lift a photograph to the nearest source of light and look through it.

This would be the one. A beast of the wild hanging full-bodied dead from his hooked fingers, sun bulging like a supercharged goiter behind them. I line it up with the light bulb behind the photograph, and several million years of light begin flowing again towards him from exactly nowhere. That manner is about him here as well, that fear more conscious of him than he is of it, so much in command of him it has taken complete ownership of his eyes.

The old farmer he stayed with, he once told me, hardly said a word. Even when they pig-dogged wild boars in the bush and dredged their bodies out of the brambles with a drag chain. The pickup kicking forward, the boars flopping in the dust. Later to hang in a barn with flies raging across their split hides. That was, according to him even now, a good memory. Context is the Holy Ghost, I should know by now, when it comes to memory. To be so at ease with myself that I could derive an apocalyptic moral from something as far gone as a photograph, my father trailing along behind it, but also, strangely, its impetus. Frightening to think he was once only twenty-three. And by that time had killed more things than I had intimate knowledge of.

I set it down, set him down. Face down. Then laugh a little. What would it cost if I were to do something as simple as take a pair of scissors and lay into it, carve a length of old color from it? Say, something that might fit convincingly over one's upper lip? It'd make an interesting portrait. A mirror, a camera, a bit of father and kangaroo and dry sunlight behind them, maybe then I might have a memento of the next arriving moment, forced into strange angles but for the purpose of looking suddenly like myself.

Who knows, it might help. It might be just the photograph to give him.

ONE FOR THE SHORT TOOTH

Yesterday I read an on-line tribute to a singer-songwriter who'd died of alcoholism, of "acute dipsomania" the guy had written, somewhat callously I thought, capitalizing on someone's last days to display his knack for writing a memorable phrase. There was nothing memorable about the way the singer had died, without medical insurance or money—he didn't even have a bank account—all of which I'm sure the reviewer writing the article *did* have. But the singer, the reviewer said, had lived along the edges he sang about, and he deliberately left it unsettled whether he thought the songs had brought the man to this condition or he had been led by simple aimlessness to write those songs. But the songs, I thought, are what the reviewer is writing about, no matter how much he describes in detail the faults and failings of the man. How little he's mentioning. Nothing about responsibility, about how loose in some ways you have to keep your commitments in order to live that kind of life, touring every six months or less. Nothing about how difficult it is to make a living now off record sales or even, for that matter, touring. About how boring constant travel can be and how it drives your talents into the realm of mere hobbies, until you're drawn to habits that are more automatic and easier to maintain, the usual ones, none too novel, drinking or drugging or burrowing through countless people's beds.

Meanwhile all the time you're getting older, "long in the tooth," a euphemism I always liked because it seems to work in the opposite direction of most euphemisms. It's more feral, uglier. More decrepit. The gums drawing back due to old age and disease and misuse so it creates the misperception it's the teeth that are actually growing longer, more fang-like. When really it's only a matter of the flesh retracting from their roots. How appropriate, I had to think, that the singer would die before he had reached forty—when the eschatological ache and the dread and the quasi-religious distortions of time and natural law in his songs would slowly draw back and become literal, a direct reference to the person who was singing them, having reached an age when it was no longer noble to be poor or aimless, without wife or house or child or belongings, a bachelor with a name and a label and a certain romanticism that people half his age force on him. There he is, losing his way every now and then on stage, forgetting very simple lyrics, his body no longer agreeing to work within the music. Which is really all that connects any of them to him anyway. Including the reviewer, who ended his piece well but still couldn't recover from the sentiments he'd sprinkled throughout like holy water where it doesn't belong, say, at an orgy or a wedding, until he reached the phrase that matters—that "he occupied the margins because the center was abhorrent." But then why would that matter, when the margins are always pulling farther and farther apart, expanding like someone's very stylized idea of a fresh stain? Not a solution or an answer but an active hallucination of a center, a place in the light, constant safety. The one that won't hold, the one that looks back. The one people write songs about thinking it will lead them back to themselves. And when it doesn't, other people, people who've heard him but don't know him, will say: well there he is, at last.

ABOUT GRIMM

After Grimm returned from Afghanistan he'd taken to stealing cars, not an easy feat in a town as small as Smithsburg; he'd rented an apartment above a feed store, visited his sister and mother, applied for jobs, was turned down by all of them, bought a small television with his first government check, bet his money dry at the Golden Mile, harness racing, the most degraded form of entertainment left over from the Roman Empire, his friend Art said, slapping his open palm with the racing form, so he was penniless that quickly, but still too proud to ask for a handout from sister or mother; he'd gone door to door in the neighborhoods where he'd grown up, offering his services as a mower of lawns and pruner of bushes, and in the two weeks only one person had taken him up on his offer, a stout, angry woman with very few teeth, who stood over him as he weeded her garden, instructing him on the proper way to grip a bundle of weeds, just so, and wriggle it, very lightly, so as to coax the roots from the ground with them, *because if you leave any shoots down in there*, she said, *more weeds are liable to grow*; no surprise he'd tire of that, lasted one afternoon then said, no more, I'll try my luck elsewhere, and in this instance he already knew luck would be found where he'd already lost it, that is, at the tracks, so he began hanging out there from mid-morning until well into the afternoon, especially on weekends, when the parking lot was as full as it was going to be, halfway at best; he'd hail people as they stepped from their cars, offer his opinion on the weather, the horses that were running that day, the jockeys, and ask, if they wouldn't mind, if he could borrow a cigarette, at least half in a sour mood but obliging him, so he'd stand there in a leisurely manner, philosophically smoking a borrowed cigarette, almost as if it were a means of marking time, which it was to a degree, because once there was only ash and filter left he'd let it drop and, taking that as his starting gun, would turn heel and ease his way between the cars, trying the door handles, and if none should give, he'd look for cracked windows, of which there were bound to be a few on such a hot day, over a hundred degrees and climbing, and through one of those cracks he'd work a little tool he'd rigged for the purpose, a coat hanger bent at the end into a taut hook, and with that lift the lock and slip in, make spaghetti with the wires under the driver's side dash, cut and splice the two that mattered, and after the engine kicked on, would listen for footsteps, and hearing none slowly, slowly ease his way up to an upright position, as natural a driver as there has ever been, and roll off with the pinched car heading across town in calm haste, making sure to cut a few loops through the surrounding neighborhoods until he'd settled on his place of destination and disappearance—a large gutted garage across from a plastics factory, where Mr. Chin, an electrician who'd been laid off from G.E. years ago, waited with the lift and tools necessary to take the whole thing apart, so he could resell them to garages around town, cheap parts, or, and this was the part that amused Grimm the most, as parts to weave back into the cars that Mr. Chin's own customers brought to him, so unbeknownst to them they were driving around with all the evidence, with the alternator or manifold or axle of their neighbors' stolen car, and Mr. Chin, who appreciated the principles of symmetry, said why not, what this place needs is fewer cars, and the ones that run at least we can make them run smoothly, besides, the cut Mr. Chin gave him was good enough to keep him coming back once or twice a month, everything simple and unassuming, until the number of allowable thefts from one parking lot was breeched and the track posted a security guard on a small stand in the middle of the lot, a kind of lifeguard, chain smoking and a surveying the lot with binoculars, of course he caught on to Grimm the first day and the next, until the third day he called him over and leaning over Grimm's head said loudly over the track announcer and the traffic, *You're either in the track or you're out, no loitering,* so off he went, corrected of his habit, at least for a day, but later in the month he found himself in a situation: rent due, his car out of gas, his refrigerator naked of food, so he left his place early and said, one more, that's it, then I'll find some better kind of employment, what, he had no idea, but it certainly wouldn't be this, where he found himself was at the gas station down the road from his place, where one or two cars rolled in every half hour to air up their tires or fill their gas, and in the shade of a large rusty propane tank alongside the station he waited, cross-legged on the ground, flicking paint chips at ants, until the right car pulled up, which, two hours later, did happen, an old woman, her grandson in the passenger's seat, they both went inside for a coffee or some candy or a hot dog and in their wake he slipped right in and caught, best of luck, her keys dangling from the ignition, and just as he started the car looked over, and in the window what did he see but the attendant, a teenage girl, haggard, the kind that's too young to be an addict but too old to still be suffering through a growing spurt, raising a thumb and smiling, but it was the wrong kind of smile, the kind that said, *Well done, asshole*; he was so surprised by that he didn't see what was over his other shoulder, so when he looked there she was, the old woman, who by then had already reached through the window to put a hand on his shoulder; he leapt like a bunch of sparks when she touched him, *Mam*, he said, in a weak voice, *I'm sorry, I think, you know I think this might not be my car, Yes*, she said, *I'd agree about that, I'm sorry to tell you it isn't,* which was a strange way to say it, that she'd caught him so early in the act he could feel some guilt about it, by then the passenger's side door was opening and the boy was sliding in, and the driver's door was opening as well, the old woman taking him by the elbow to help him out, so within seconds he was standing there with the woman looking up at him, the sun in his eyes, embarrassment already warm in his stomach, and she asked the most unlikely thing, so direct and unremarkable he had to answer, *Well, do you want a ride, we'll drive you wherever you're going*, to which he said, *Sure, that's just what I need, but I'm not sure where that'd be*, the old woman laughing as he took the back seat, so clean and spacious he was sure he could lie down, long and wide enough to hold a man, if not comfortable enough to keep him there.

STORIES ON THE HALF SHELL

1) *Polish Salt Mine.* A young woman, Poltana, carries liquor in a wicker picnic basket down to the men who work in a large salt mine (modeled after Wieliczka). In a small tin container slung around her shoulder by a leather strap, she carries hosts blessed by the village priest. There's a chapel made of chiseled salt half a mile below: altar, relief sculpture, pews. The miners hold mass there. Gradually they begin to worship a sodium deity, an earth spirit. The girl's brother works in the mines. He explains that this is an "inverted church"; just as every tree near a lake extends its depth in a reflection, this underground church is the reflection of the village cathedral. At the end of the story, the church begins to sink into the ground, because the ground beneath it has been hollowed out by all the salt that has been mined below. The whole church settles into the sinkhole with its spires still poking out of the ground like trees. Come winter, the men of the village fell them with crosscut saws and use them as firewood.

2) *The Snow Therapist*. An older man, a septuagenarian, visits a YMCA in Cabrini Greene every week. He sits at a cafeteria table sipping gas station coffee from a Styrofoam cup, watching the boys play basketball and the girls play Marco Polo and skip rope. He strikes up conversation with some of the boys; they're confrontational, disrespectful, but he asks them a few odd-sounding questions about their home lives; they begin to listen. He is a snow therapist. Walks kids onto the playground/park and has them watch the snow for five minutes, then ten minutes, then a half hour each day. The kids get calmer, quieter. Then spring comes, and they try watching rain, but it doesn't have the same effect, and gradually the angst they were carrying around begins to slip into view again.

3) *Last Days of Laika*. Rocket scientists' pampering of Laika days before she's launched into orbit. One of them takes her home to play with his children the day before the launch. They gave her nicknames, "Zhuchka," "Limonchik." Maybe write it as an epistolary, a letter from one of the scientists to Laika. A stray husky mix found on the streets of Moscow, in winter. Describe her tests, her training, the launch, then imagine her experience in the cabin of the rocket, her heart-attack, what it must have been like orbiting the earth dead. Then describe in an apologetic way what it must have been like during reentry, when she was reduced to ash and dispersed into the earth's atmosphere, more cloud than dog.

4) *Mama Pia*. An ex-drug addict and his girlfriend, a Bulgarian ex-policewoman and classically trained cellist, are invited by her friend Eduardo to attend a peyote ritual in a cabin outside Pittsburgh.

They arrive in the late afternoon and enter a hardfloor room with a fireplace. Forty other people are there. Mike Donner, the owner of cabin and host, welcomes people; Mama Pia, the Mexican woman, sits with her friend on the windowsill, her bags and sleeping roll at her feet. She has a cache of long dried tobacco stalks. She begins the ritual by throwing the stalks on the fire, chanting. There's no sense that this is an authentic ritual. She brews peyote buttons in boiled water. Everyone has a cup next to them and lifts it to be filled. She instructs them not to gulp it down: sip. They sip and many of them go to the bathroom to vomit. Then they sit again cross-legged on the floor and have their hallucinations. Not pleasurable, just distortions of sense perceptions. He has hallucinations of dead friends, and of himself dead those years he lived with the woman he was an addict with, of himself in inpatient rehab, of the woman musician he went on tour with and who put a curse on him in the Mojave Desert, of himself as his girlfriend's dead husband, a policeman in Bulgaria. He realizes he is her dead husband inhabiting the body of an American man ten years younger. The next day, the sadness he feels driving home under the trees, in the spring, with her groggy beside him. That feeling of not being the man she loved, but of also being him.

5) *Midnight Negatives.* Story about the Union Carbide plant in Paducah. Narrated in the first person plural by radioactive isotopes. Describe how they damage the cells of different townspeople and workers in the plant and how they enter the atmosphere when uranium-laced steam is released from the cooling towers. These confidential company files call, when they're unearthed years later,

"Midnight Negatives." Between 1952 and 1989, an estimated 66 tons of them are released into the sky, raining down for miles and miles as a million indescribable narrators.

6) *The Pursuer*. James Booker a la Cortázar. Story about Booker's last days in New Orleans, playing sets at the Maple Leaf Lounge. His schizophrenia and heroin addiction, and the lucid moment an interviewer once recorded when, in the middle of a jumbled rant, he stopped, looked up, and said to him in a very even, despairing tone: "I'm a lonely motherfucker." Based off of Cortázar's portrait of Charlie Parker. Narrated from the viewpoint of the interviewer, some guy from New York.

7) *Ceauşescu's Telephone*. About a woman who returns to her mother's apartment in Bucharest to pack up her things and either donate them or put them in storage. Her brother is in his residency at a hospital in Chicago and will fly home after the funeral to help her pack. She's a computer programmer in her 30's living in Iaşi. Before her mother lived in the apartment, her grandmother lived there. Both women lost their husbands early on, her father to alcoholism, her grandfather to the regime's investigations of anti-government activities. The main character, Adela, notices a large black rotary telephone on the kitchen counter next to an out-of-date looking microwave. She notices its cord leads straight into the wall, no jack. This telephone, she remembers, was a family legend—the "Twenty Year Telephone." Her grandmother had applied to the government-run phone company for a phone installation in the 60's, but it didn't arrive until after she had died, in the mid-80's. Her

mother had kept it around the apartment as a joke and a tribute to Ceaușescu's regime. While meeting up around town with her old school friend Milena, she begins boxing the contents of her mother's closets. The phone begins to ring at night. Adela misses the caller a few times but one day answers it. A man and woman moaning in pain. She answers again: Elena Ceaușescu. The wife of the President is protesting against someone who is binding her hands and feet. She's repeating or reliving what happened after her and her husband's mock trial. She doesn't hear Adela speaking to her. Next time she answers the phone, it's Ceaușescu himself. He's protesting the charges against him. Adela argues with him, but he can't hear, so she begins to speak and behave and ask the questions of the men who had cross-examined him during his trial. He begins to answer and argue, and she begins to change the direction of the examination until she finally gets him to admit he had no sense of the consequences of his policies. The story ends with Adela hanging up the phone to him crying, "I'm dying, I'm dying." With a kitchen knife she cuts the cord to the phone and drops it in the trash can.

FROM ANNA

On television last night, in a hotel room, downtown Chicago, the Ohio House, nearly two hundred channels but we settle on two men fighting in a cage. An Ultimate Fighting match held in—where is it, Terre Haute?—the taller of the two men squeezing the other breathless in a leg lock. Next, we're told, two women, Zoltana Spruce and Pam Hollander-Johnson, will meet for their third match in as many years. A close-up before a commercial catches Zoltana chewing her mouthpiece; it might as well have been a human ear.

Soon they'll beat each other half dead and it's almost certain we'll laugh.

Stimulated by the bloodshed (admittedly minor, not like in the old days), Anna will rest her bourbon and ginger on her stomach and make use of her extensive learning. Women fought for the Romans, she'll tell me. She'll be disgusted that I've made her watch this, so of course she'll bring the Romans into it. She'll mention Commodius or some other horrible specimen of cruelty; she'll describe women and children forced to fight wild animals in the Coliseum; and with Zoltana in view will recall mention of an Ethiopian woman of the 1st Century who killed seven men in combat before she was slain against the people's wishes. It's her area of knowledge, but I will take pains to remind her, I'm holding the remote. One flick of the channel and no more history.

A long day behind us; several hundred miles of road passing through us like the worst kind of tapeworm. Anna's head bobs, her chin tapping her chest, pulling up fresh again. We've been drinking as if we're angry at travel, but there's so much sleep ahead it'd take nothing short of a fistfight to keep us watching. Zoltana stands covered in blood. A referee lifts her arm; she's so exhausted she doesn't realize she's won until her arm is up. Of course that's an exaggeration. I'm not a historian, I see blood and assume the worst.

The room is quiet a long while then Anna clinks her drink on the nightstand. Raised from sleep, she keeps talking. She talks a long while and it's so easy to follow I begin to suspect I'm dreaming; when's the last time I've lost all sense of myself, fallen into a steady advance of words like this? Anna is telling the room about something she read once. She moves forward, the television lights the way, she keeps talking.

"More than two thousand years, that's crazy. And that's just what there's a record of. That kind of thing doesn't just come from nowhere. It didn't even begin with the Romans. The Etruscans had a hand in it even before them. I mean, wherever there're more than enough slaves, why not? There's such a thing as *too many* slaves." I laughed. Right there, that was Anna's humor. Precise to the point of ugliness.

"The craziest thing I'd ever heard, though, was from this

anthropologist my sister and I met during a work function in Belize. He'd done ten years of work in Turkey; in fact, I think he might have been Turkish. Maybe not. Maybe he'd just lost all his white back there, who knows, assimilation goes both ways.

"He'd done work in the north, along the Black Sea. The Roman era. Northern Galitia and Cappadocia, some digs along the border, what had been, back in 1 B.C., 1 A.D., the Kingdom of Armenia.

"There was a small kingdom, I don't remember the name of it, apparently it hadn't lasted too long. No one had been looking for it, basically because, though there'd been mention of it in old Roman tax records, no one had found any evidence it had existed. Not one building, no sarcophagi or burial dumps or city remains. But their third summer digging they found something—a large stone-lined pit. When they kept at it, they found themselves standing at the center of a large stadium carved partially in the ground. Load-bearing post-holes had been found at regular intervals around it. These, they guessed, could have been base structures for wooden bleachers. There was no record of a Roman stadium in that area that long ago. At most a couple of barracks. There'd been no uprisings in that region; mostly the Romans had concentrated on the easternmost and northern territories.

"Later that summer they found the first graves. Right under the stadium floor. They realized quickly enough it wasn't a matter of one grave or another—all of them eventually linked up. What they had on their hands was one large mass grave. Which was very un-Roman. If the stadium was used for fighting, then they must have fought over fresh graves. You could even imagine them stamping down the ground as they ran over it.

"There must have been hundreds of bodies. Maybe thousands. Difficult to tell, so many of the bones were cluttered together in a mess. For all they knew it could have been an infinite number of bones belonging to a single body, some naked sleeping giant the crows had picked apart.

"It wasn't until they began to remove the bones and tag them that they realized how much of a slaughter they had on their hands. How could so many have died in one place with no record of it? The condition of the bones suggested violent deaths—many cut, snapped or sharply fractured. They sent a few back to a lab in England to have them identified and dated. When word came back, they were even more confused but mostly just horrified.

"All bones belonged to males or females over fifty years of age. Fifty at that time was beyond old. Their first-look assessments were confirmed, too, on the manner of death. Blunt trauma, many of them. Others, death by sword, spear, or knife.

"A larger shipment of remains sent to the lab came back with the same: all had belonged to people, mostly women, well past child bearing age.

"What had happened there, in that arena, had only involved the old, and the evidence pointed pretty clearly to something impossible, or if not impossible, until then something completely unheard of. Here there had been gladiatorial contests of some sort, and only the elderly were buried, so it might stand to rest that only the elderly were set against each other in contest. Chew on that. Think about it. Zoltana looks pretty lucky now, doesn't she?

"Very lucky. Because get this. They figured, why were they fighting if they weren't *forced* to fight, these old people? There were very few records of the people in this kingdom, it didn't last long and considering what they found there, it wasn't a mystery why. But what little they did know didn't suggest they were particularly violent. No more than the other cultures in the region. Really, the Romans were far and away the most savage. So it might have been a Roman influence.

"Then, on some bit of stone they found in the dig, they found something written, in Latin actually. And what it said was what they'd actually come to suspect—that these old people were people from the city and maybe the outlying villages. According to custom they were gathered into the arena and given weapons of their choice and were forced to fight to the death. On a tablet later found beneath the bleachers certain penalties were mentioned. Should a gladiator choose not to fight, or decide to kill herself, her youngest grandchild would be killed. For every competitor she killed, she was granted another year of life. This law applied to all citizens beginning on their fiftieth year. The implications were pretty clear. Here was a culture even more severe than the Romans."

I had watched Anna the whole time she spoke. Not once did it seem she wasn't sleeping. That loll of the head, hands folded limply across her belly—but no, she was severely awake and speaking, at least it seemed, directly to the television. A commercial for Lays potato chips mutated into an ad for a cell phone provider. The ambiguity broke when her mouth spread widely, gradually open into a yawn, a lion's yawn.

"How many people that age, do you imagine, are sleeping right now in Chicago?"

I chuckled. The television flashed. A new commercial.

"No, really. Count them on your fingers—how many?"

AHEAD

Think of the Arabian Nights, all one thousand and one of them, but imagine Schehrezade and Shahryar, the storyteller and the listener, as one person, one person telling stories to stay her execution, her executioner listening so close to her they just so happen to be enclosed in the same head. That's me, here, right now, gun to my head. This is how poor I am with details: even if I turned the gun over in my hands and looked, I couldn't tell you what make or model it is. It's the gun that's going to draw a straight line right through my head, that's all, threading a bullet through the heads of both the king and his wily mistress on its way out the other end.

What brought him to this? someone asks—I can already hear them. What sat him in that chair in his basement with the lights out and made him put a gun to his right temple? Why not put it to the roof of his mouth? Why not press it under the chin? The place someone chooses to be the entry point of a fatal bullet must have some symbolic significance. It can't be entirely random. If there are specific reasons that drove him to sit himself there, in his basement, in a wicker backed chair given to him by his grandmother, alone, in a house on which a second straight night of rain was falling, the lights out, the gun dark and gleaming, its muzzle pressed lightly at his right temple, all of these facts must be specifically chosen for the purpose, correct? They must bear some combined significance. After all, it could have easily been a sunny afternoon he'd chosen, basking in a lawn chair on his sun deck, well-tanned with a half-full Cuba Libre in hand (as opposed, of course, to a half-empty one).

No, his end, *my* end, was specific, obliquely unforgiving, a definite act, a forceful way of tying up certain facts within the world and making them come to nothing. But things have not come to that, not yet; I'm still sitting here, eyes closed, the metal at my temple as innocent of its potential as a grain of sand (but then, who would think to thank a grain of sand for its innocence).

Initially my promise to myself was to pull the trigger once there was nothing else to think about—only that one small act, the contraction of my right index finger half an inch towards its palm, bringing the trigger with it. That's what had put me here anyways: too much in the head, too much moving around. The best way to put a little stillness in it is to make a hole, one that runs from one end to the other—so the busy pollutants inside can rush out. To produce a genie from a bottle, all one has to do is rub it. But the same doesn't go for one's own head. Rubbing doesn't help, nor does knocking it, nor does cracking it against doorframes do much good. Any kind of work you do on the outside only reinforces the constipation inside of it. No, the best way to get any relief is to treat your head like a lamp or a bottle, some proper vessel for a wish-granting spirit: to rub the muzzle of a gun borrowed from your brother ever so lightly against your temple. Not the left temple, mind you; that would be bad luck. The right one, the one that bears the ear that listens over the shoulder of a god only fifteen percent of the population believes in anymore.

The sounds you hear, I hear: rainwater splattering on the sidewalk beside the basement window.

So I tell myself stories. Every last story I can remember. Every one anyone ever told me, in every variation that I retold them. From childhood through the successive failures of my twenties, all the way until now, in the full flower of my obscurity to others and to myself: all the stories that led from then until now. Once I had exhausted them—because there is an end to such stories, stories that reality brings to a person, to plant in them and flower in some other, more engorged, more exaggerated manner—I moved on to those bits and pieces of events that had and hadn't happened. Those hybrid exploits one recounts by accident, when one's mind is distracted or bored or overly enamored with the uncanniness of imagined details. This and this happened (though it didn't), this was the result (though it wasn't). It went on like this for hours, for days. I sat there, the gun almost an afterthought, a prop to my own talking to myself, telling lies to see how well they sound when I elaborate on them, that is, as they say, "stretch" them, elastic as they are, like life, the very kind I was threatening to snap and put an end to. What was amazing was that, no matter how far I stretched them, the truths of these stories I was making up would always give way a little more, more and more, until it seemed no amount of pressure would break them. Stories of women and men throughout every period of history; stories of mythological beings in compromising dilemmas; stories of war and rape and infatuation and grief and whimsical insinuations—every manner of character and conflict, every possible scenario in which reality as one lived it might cut its teeth. All of life and death was but a babe, I thought, and this gun, really, is the most nourishing thing, no, not even a bottle but the breast itself, a nipple—which most vital forces imaginable instinctually reach to suckle on.

As you can tell, I was too occupied to do anything but listen, marveling at the slippage of my own mind. Was this evidence that I wanted to live, or, more specifically, that something within me—more vital than myself—didn't want to die? Yes, and yes. And even the gun and all five bullets lying dumb in its clip agreed: what they could so easily put an end to they couldn't even begin to explain. And so, to torture the gun, to testify to its own impotence, that voice in my head and that other energy within it, the one that listened, enraptured at the twists and turns of their own inventions and bold sensual lies, continued to feed each other, more sleepless and relentless than an Arabian Night. As if the very strength of their collaboration were enough to reignite the dead, the hundreds of dead virgins who had paved the way to this one morning, the morning after, in this chair, this chair after I had risen from it, tired, happy, exhausted but fulfilled, confused that the uselessness of a weapon in my hand could seem so genial as I pocketed it.

As I climb the stairs, the light outside, because I'm already describing it (to myself and to myself listening) is twice as wild as any sun.

As long as I climb, it keeps shining.

ACKNOWLEDGMENTS

SPRING IN ZURVEYTA draws some of its details and dialogue from accounts described in Anna Politkovskaya's *Russian Diary: A Journalist's Final Account of Life, Corruption, and Death in Putin's Russia.*

Thanks to Carolee Schneemann and Dick Higgins for their LOST DANCES.

Kyle Coma-Thompson lives in Louisville, Kentucky.